DESTROYER

CLAYTON LINDEMUTH

DESTROYER

CLAYTON LINDEMUTH
HARDGRAVE ENTERPRISES LLC
SAINT CHARLES, MISSOURI

COPYRIGHT © 2021 BY CLAYTON LINDEMUTH.

PUBLISHED BY HARDGRAVE ENTERPRISES LLC AND CLAYTON LINDEMUTH.

CLAYTON LINDEMUTH ASSERTS HIS MORAL RIGHTS AS AUTHOR OF DESTROYER.

ALL RIGHTS RESERVED. NO PART OF THIS PUBLICATION MAY BE REPRODUCED, DISTRIBUTED OR TRANSMITTED IN ANY FORM OR BY ANY MEANS, INCLUDING PHOTOCOPYING, RECORDING, OR OTHER ELECTRONIC OR MECHANICAL METHODS, WITHOUT THE PRIOR WRITTEN PERMISSION OF THE PUBLISHER, EXCEPT IN THE CASE OF BRIEF QUOTATIONS EMBODIED IN CRITICAL REVIEWS AND CERTAIN OTHER NONCOMMERCIAL USES PERMITTED BY COPYRIGHT LAW. FOR PERMISSION REQUESTS, WRITE TO THE PUBLISHER, ADDRESSED "ATTENTION: PERMISSIONS COORDINATOR," AT CLAYLINDEMUTH@GMAIL.COM. NAH, JUST KIDDING. SEND IT TO CLAYTON.

EDITED BY GAIL LAMBERT

PUBLISHER'S NOTE: THIS IS A WORK OF FICTION. NAMES, CHARACTERS, PLACES, AND INCIDENTS ARE A PRODUCT OF THE AUTHOR'S IMAGINATION. LOCALES AND PUBLIC NAMES ARE SOMETIMES USED FOR ATMOSPHERIC PURPOSES. ANY RESEMBLANCE TO ACTUAL PEOPLE, LIVING OR DEAD, OR TO BUSINESSES, COMPANIES, EVENTS, INSTITUTIONS, OR LOCALES IS COMPLETELY COINCIDENTAL.

DESTROYER/CLAYTON LINDEMUTH

ISBN: 9798491149261

ALSO BY CLAYTON LINDEMUTH

TREAD

Solomon Bull

Cold Quiet Country

Strong at the Broken Places

Sometimes Bone

Nothing Save the Bones Inside Her

My Brother's Destroyer

The Mundane Work of Vengeance

Pretty Like an Ugly Girl

The Outlaw Stinky Joe

Blunt Force Kindness

The Men I sent Forward

Shirley F'N Lyle: VIVA the Revolution

Shirley F'N Lyle: One at a Time, Boys

Shirley F'N Lyle: Totally Sunshine and Love

FOR BETTYE THORNTON

The way you faced your troubles and broken heart with joy inspired us.

May you find peace with your love, who preceded you.

THANK YOU,

Cindy Wasson, for suggesting Baer's memory that he was in love with her.

Andy and Pat Patton for suggesting Baer dreaming of a 1965 International D1100.

Aleta Babcock Haase for the idea the truck had a log book in the glove box, detailing every single mile driven by the truck.

Edie Knisell for the idea of sitting in the back of the truck while it bounced up a hill.

Sue Doucette for the name and backstory for Heidi "Press" Stone.

For Editing

Gail Lamber

Chrystal Wilkins

For Beta Reading:

Ralph Bush
Rachell Horbenko
Dub Hedgeglass
Kathie Marold
Cindy Wasson
Karl Hughey
Anthony Goodner

CHAPTER ONE

Night. Got a gold coin in hand. They's three men on short logs 'round the fire. The one with the guitar don't see but the other two is spooked. They pull pistols and hunch...

But these Ohio flatlanders won't see me lookin' that a way.

I use numbnuts' soarin' rendition of some bullshit tune I heard one time when I had a radio to skitter close and once these boys realize they left the angle unwatched, they'll turn and spot me. But it won't do 'em no good.

Why wait?

"Howdy."

I wave my hand and maybe the gold glints in the firelight and catch their attention. Smith ain't yet come out his leather and if a pistol had a mood, I'd say my .44's mostly uninterested.

But the two pistols on me seem lively. No waver, just steady lines on my guts and this is the part I like.

All these times since I become the law, the wicked see me, but it's like they's thinkin' through a headache or swimmin' in tar. And me sharp as a whittled stick. I feel the juice and it don't bother me so much as stiffen the spine and put a razor edge on my thinkin', keep me cuttin' the future a second afore the folk around me. Fuckin' uncanny bein' on the right side of the self. These boys' eyes glow like cherry coals, but grayed over with ash and though it's all on cue, I don't take a thing for granted. Not how the pistol hands stay true. Not how the guitar man's already shifted feet twice. Not how the one on the right got his head cocked left, like to hear. He'll be the last to move and when things go to shit he'll be the first to try a sucker move.

I see it all like I'm a magnifyin' glass born to spot evil.

"Hey, you fella with the guitar there. How 'bout you pick me a song?"

"This dude's on crack."

"Or you want I should pay the piper, 'fore I call the tune?"

I chuck the gold piece.

"Like, what the fuck?"

"Son," I stretch out the arm and step close and the gun barrels follow — and if these boys is swimmin' in tar, they's maybe use to the viscosity or on the college swim team. "Son, nobody says *like* these days. Even when you and your girlfriends thought it was groovy, it wasn't." I close in like to take the young maestro under wing but cuff him 'cross the jaw instead. Open hand with a big bang but little sting 'cept the embarrassment. He look like a wrestler, maybe, way the neck veins go apeshit. A swimmer-wrestler. College stud. "Listen, son, if you got ears to hear."

"What the fuck?" says one to the other and the other look back.

Says I, "I want you to play me the song you did for that girl. You know."

Six eyes is pure red, little suns of hate.

"The girl?"

"Uh-huh."

"What girl? What are you talking about?"

"Dude — what girl?"

"Don't be coy," says I. "I got a lotta humor for a wanderin' lawman but untruth ain't comedic, see? I'm liable to cut things short and you won't get the full ballyhoo with the sendoff. You won't get the explanation you want, and while they's no rule says I got to send you forward any particular way, it don't feel right nor just without the ballyhoo."

Fella with the guitar is red in the eyes and red on both cheeks but redder on the one I struck. He clench his teeth then says through 'em: "What girl?"

"It was six month back in this very neck o' wood. Y'all took turns, and way she tell it, you there with the guitar — you kept strummin' while the other two shamed all Ohio, what they did to her. Then you took your turn and said the song words in her ear. You was drunk, she put in the diary. So much you couldn't finish. You just slap her face 'til her lip bleed, and roll off. That is, accordin' to her diary."

"I don't know what you're talking about."

He spits and starts easin' the guitar over his head to free himself of the strap.

Says I, "I bet sober you're the sort likes to pee on the porcelain, so no one hear the noise."

"I want some of what he's smokin'. The balls on this guy."

"No shit, right?"

"Boys, boys. You'll be tangled up in the same mystery as me

in due time. Short time — so let's focus and knock this part out. As I was sayin', Guitar Man, she put it all in her diary and you knew that. So when she took the pills it was you that took the book and hid it. Right so far?"

He stoop slow and set the guitar neck to lean on the log that held his ass. Cracks his knuckles 'cause he seen it on TV.

The other two step aside and next they'll want to make a circle and close in. How they always do.

"Easy, boys. I know you got the guns out and all, but if you think on it you don't want to circle up on me. They's no crossfire if y'all shoot one direction."

Fella on the right blinks hard and still got no clue. One on the left nods slow and stops steppin'. Guitar Man lowers the forehead a inch so his face is half fire light and half shadow.

"What's your angle? What you want?"

I smile. Beam.

Says I, "Your stepsister ran from this life 'cause you chased her out. You took the book, easy as doin' a little snoopin'. And you thought you was safe."

I wait. Let him noodle it. But longer I wait, more heat come off they eyes 'n the fire.

Says I, "Was it the devil on your right shoulder or the one on the left that told?"

"Told who?"

"Ah. If you knew that, you'd know it all."

"Let's just kill him," says the one on the left.

I smile. Beam. Glow. Raise the brows and rotate the eyeballs left. Wink.

Guitar Man turns right. "The fuck, Monk? Who'd you tell?"

"I didn't tell no one."

Now he's shootin' red at Guitar Man. A real live wire and

Guitar Man don't see the red nor feel the juice, as he's blind to the evil he swim in.

Says I, "You told your older brother, Monk... But you ain't been keepin' up with his life these last few years, what with all the warfare in his soul. He been through some highs and lows and found the Lord at the bottom. Then lost him and wanted to find him agin — so it was an accident we met. Him in the bar lookin' fer the Lord and me lookin' Wild Turkey. Your brother's a tormented man, Monk, and you drop a doozy on him. He confess his troubles on me, maybe thinkin' no man's ever gonna right a wrong in a town he don't know or give a shit about. And that was his mistake and yours. And all yours. So here we are. Y'all took the odds when it was three agin a sixteen-year-old girl. How 'bout three to me, you fuckin' pussies."

Blank stares.

"Stop," says Guitar Man. "You read the diary?"

"Uh-huh. If she was alive, it'd been different. But you go to that Google place and her name come right up with the sad news."

"How'd you get the diary?"

"I'm in good with a thief."

One set a eyeballs twist, another and the last, 'til all three men's eyes is on each other's. I watch and once the eyeballs click off each other and back on me, see the feet's now in control. Three men rotate heels then toes 'til each is situated just how he think 'll best advantage 'im. And while I was watchin' the feet, I see how each drop the ass a few inch. Bend the knees. Spread the arms and rotate shoulders like birds set to wing.

These fellers ain't in tar.

"Looks like y'all's ready for the ballyhoo. Here goes. You don't know it, but none of this shit's real. I keep sayin' it and no one ever gits it. But these trees, that fire, you and me: we're all low order. We don't know the stuff we're in or the stuff we're made a. All this is natural — don't misunderstand. But in the higher order we're just fart smoke, right? Dream stuff."

"I think he's high on something."

"Dude, like, we have guns on you."

"No, like, lissen. You might be a dude and these girls with you. But I ain't a dude. I am the law you broke come back to haunt your ass and set things right. Send you forward so you can get the Almighty's recap and be about your merry way in the nonlocal."

"He is definitely tripping."

"Shoot him — right? Should we?"

"Maybe beat him."

"But he knows about Sue."

"Why'd you go and say her name?"

"Uh. He already read her diary. We have to shoot him."

"No — those lights over there are houses."

"Y'all could stone me like they did in the Old Book."

"That's a good idea."

"Wow, you know that could work."

"Yeah, what?"

"Accourse, you got to think 'bout the blood. You'd have to stand back fifteen feet. I'm a bleeder, see. But wily and quick — you might step back fifteen feet and I ske-daddle while you're still weighin' rocks for one won't hurt your arm. Specially you, non-bicep fucker."

"He's right. You have skinny arms. We have to be close."

"Pardon me, mister, but how come you're helpin' us out, and all?"

"Well boys, we got work to do. No need to act unfriendly or whatever."

"Yeah, cool."

"So, while y'all was thinkin' there, I come up with the solution."

"What's that?"

"I'm just gonna go ahead and — "

Noise to the right ain't right. What —

Cock the ear. Let the fingers shift Smithward. Eyeballs flit —

Feet on the left. I cut back the head and twist the eyeballs and yank at Smith but that cocky fuck on the left drive his skull right through my chest. We both fly back and all I wonder is where's the last log I stepped over? Was it here, like to bust out my brain? Or one step back, where maybe I can wrestle this prick and bust his?

We land and it was neither, but I catch a good rock to the ribs. Prick's rearin' back to start punchin' and they's a zap, splash and pistol bang and all the boy's brain-stuff is mist and chunks.

"Fuck."

Now he's got the red fountain splashin' blood; heart ain't yet heard the bad news. I roll afore he drop on me.

Zap! Splash! Pistol bang!

Guitar man's knees buckle and he drops.

"Good girl, Tat."

"Tat?" says the skinny-armed coward I called for the sucker punch.

"Don't worry 'bout Tat. She's a good shot. You won't see

nor hear it comin'. But I want to tell you what to expect. — Tat! Hold off a minute, aright? — She gets impatient. More and more these last few days. Irritable. Anyhow, see, it's like I was sayin' afore. You're like a television set. The signal's out there but the picture's in the box. Well, you're goin' home to where the signal come from."

"You mean the tower?"

"Uh, well shit. I ain't thought of it. Maybe if the tower's in space or somethin'. Tell you what, you'll know soon enough anyway and once I figure it out — "

Zap! Splash! Pistol bang!

" — I'll be sure to tell the next feller. Shit. Tat? I was talkin'."

She step out from behint a giant beech. "That is all you do. Let's go. Punch and move."

Stinky Joe crash through some brush and sniff the guitar on the log.

"Punch and move. I do say that a lot. But maybe we oughta sort this out."

"Okay, fine. You want to die or something?"

"Uh. Not I was aware."

"Wonderful. You're just stupid."

Her eyes is glassy in the campfire. "That needs a log."

"No it don't. We ain't stayin'."

Tat gimme a grimace like to carve in a pumpkin and hold it while she close with. One foot off, nearly eye to eye as she's on a rock, she take my right hand, unfurl the fingers and slap her belly. Press it tight.

I pull back.

She yank my hand back in place.

"What?" says I.

"What?" She leers.

"I'm missin' this whole thing here. What you got in mind, Tat? You want some action by the fire? Kinda weird with all the dead men so close... Fuck it. I'm game."

"What do you feel?"

"Woman. Nice woman."

"That is your baby, Baer."

CHAPTER TWO

Tat's in the back seat asleep and Joe's curled on the front passenger side. Each time I hit a pothole or a patch a blacktop on the cement interstate, such as they's so fond of in Ohio, Joe open his eyes and stare like I woke 'im on purpose.

Fifty-three-year-old.

Fifty-three and Tat's knocked up. She was eighteen when she first mount Little Big Baer that night in the cave. Now she's eighteen and a half.

"Fifty-three," says I, quiet so Tat don't rouse.

Fuck.

Fuck!

If I was layin' in the sleep sack I wouldn't sleep so may 's well get some miles... if I gotta be fifty-fuckin'-three.

Stinky Joe got his eyes closed.

He say, *There is an alternative.*

"Fifty-four?"

You could be dead.

"Truer words's never spoke — though I don't know why I'm talkin' at a dog won't look at the fella he's conversatin' with. It ain't couth."

There's a word for that. Besides... when in Rome...

"Ah, now see, that's bullshit. I got my eyes open wide. Seein' all — sometimes a second or two ahead. Sometimes it's like I wouldn't even need the eyes, I get the vision so clear."

Exactly.

Joe don't open his eyes, so I don't got to make my face look like what he said make sense.

"What are you talking about?" says Tat.

"Go back to sleep. It's Joe up here runnin' his mouth."

I flip the high beams. Take the left lane to keep roadkill off the wheels and undercarriage. Switch back to the right.

After a hundred mile or so, the thought occurs I got as many days ahead as I had when I was born, as the day I first felt the juice, as the day I become the law: none. I got no days ahead. No minutes nor seconds ahead. Truth is no man's got more 'n the moment he occupy, the foot where he stands, the air in his lungs the moment he suck it in. No bullet but what's in the chamber... and that satisfies like a cool drink for a tired soul, as I got the same future with that baby as if I was same age as Tat: unknown.

Drive five hours on whatever interstate's handy. Too many for a reasonable man to choose, so I stick with the even numbers or if both is even, the one exits right. The 76, then the 80. Skip the 79. Odd numbers always sorta piss me off, but it's so far down the catalog I never ponder why.

I sip coffee and fist the eyeballs when they misbehave, but by and by I wake on the rumble strip and figger it's better to keep dyin' slow rather'n all at once, so I take the very next exit, a rest stop a couple hours into Pennsylvania.

Never been so deep in Yank territory. Don't 'xactly call myself a Reb, but growin' up learnin' the battles took place in the War of Northern Aggression I half wonder if they's Union troops in the weeds. Five A.M... A man'll think up anything at all.

Fifty-fuckin'-three.

Yeah, but I could die right now like Stinky Joe say, and it'd all be good.

Rest area sign points right for cars and left for trucks. Cut the wheel and tap the brake and ahead is two cops parked side by side and if it wouldn't look curious, I'd tool on past and get back on the highway. But I trust the Almighty to hex these lawmen long enough I can splash some water on the face and pinch my ear. I'll find rest for the night at the next exit — it's been off-ramps every ten mile for two hour.

Ease into the slot at the end where dogs is free to mess the grass. Engine off, I sit with eyes shut and dotted yellow lines flashin' in the mind. Morse code it's the — for T, — — for M, and — — — for O. Like the highway says Tom over and over. Or Mot. TMO. OMT. Ain't a helluva lot to work with. In numbers it's — — — — — for zero, and that seem a better fit. Endless zeros.

What I'd give for a couple dots, is all. Big round ones, bury my face in.

Exit, ease the door shut and press 'til it click. In and out, splash the head and soak the face. Pinch the ear. Take a leak. Choke on raw stink from some feller in the shitter one more fart from losin' his life and don't know it. But conscience gimme a nudge: killin' ain't suitable.

"Hey."

Nothin'.

"Hey you in the shitter."

"Unh? Yeah."

"You need an ambulance? Can you walk — or d' you blow your whole backside off?"

"Sure, I can walk. Oh — yeah, that's funny. Stinks pretty good, right?"

"A fine achievement. Safe travels. You set a new mark."

"How so?"

"How rotten your ass is. Maybe a new mark on the wall too."

Outside the doors I stop and fill the lungs with Pennsylvania air. It's as close to North Carolina where I grew up as any I smell since I been on the run. I recall Mae choppin' my hair at the Hardees there in Kentucky. I scoop some that dirt and give it a whiff. And there in Colorado runnin' and slippin' in the snow and mud out by the organic dope farmers, I know exactly what Glenwood Springs smell like under the skirt. Arizona don't smell so much as saunter in dry and clean, make anyplace at all good for a stretch and snooze, so long as it's under shade. But this Pennsylvania air's back the other way toward North Carolina. Fella'd expect a handful of mud if he slap the air.

Eyes is tired agin', already. Shoulda put my mouth to the faucet. I stop and turn but voices roll 'cross the blacktop. Cops is still there, windows down and lights off. I'll get my liquid in the form of Turkey.

Back in the car I ease the door gentle but Tat rolls on the back seat.

"Where are we?"

"Pennsylvania."

"What's in Pennsylvania?"

"Dutch."

"What's Dutch?"

"You got the ovens, for starts. Then the people. You got the Dutch mother tongue, which is Kraut. Hell if I know. And they got the horses and buggies. Anyway, you'll like to need the toilet, now yer pregnant."

I chin at the building. "Rest stop."

"What does that have to do with anything?"

"What's what?"

"Now that I'm pregnant."

"Don't pregnant gals pee a lot? All the pressure?"

"You weren't being smart?"

"Ain't capable. You can use the toilet or wait. Was thinkin' we might sleep here but with them cops over there I'll grab the next exit and park in the trees somewhere."

She exhales hard. Rest her head on the window.

"What time is it?"

"Almost light."

Head shake, paired with a frown.

"Call it five."

She close her eyes and drop back on the seat. I fire the engine and cruise out. Turn signal for the on-ramp. The sign say seventy but I'll keep her at sixty five 'til I know Yanks better.

Four mile and it's the Dubois Airport exit. Lookin' left and right, the left got houses in view and the right don't, so I spin the wheel clockwise and after a half mile it's dark all 'bout.

Pass a red, white and blue election sign, in the shape of a hand with a raised middle finger. One sign out alone, wavin' the bird. Elect Levi Hardgrave. Need bigger letters. Or less dark at night.

This many trees, they's bound to be a forest road, a loggin' road, farmer's road or somethin'. I keep it under twenty and in a mile spot a downhill left givin' out to gravel then dirt. In a hundred yards the bottom go flat. They's a bridge over a stream suitable for trout and firewood all about. On the left the trees clear out a little so the morning gray drips in the hollow. Loggin' road's built up with stone the first twenty feet, and after that it's mangled land ripped up by ten-foot tires and thousand-horse engines.

LAND FOR SALE
814-555-5239

I PULL FORWARD, THEN BACK IN WATCHIN' THE MIRRORS AND when the transmission's in park and the engine's off and tickin', I let the eyelids settle and my head drop back on the seat. I got a sweaty neck and don't care for it. Crack the window and it's warmer out 'n in. Close the eyes and listen to the ears ring. Tat sighs. Stinky Joe whisper farts and reachin' for the passenger window I second think it. Draft could blow in like as out.

Fifty-three.

Tat moans. Giggles.

Agin I crack the latch and ease out the vehicle. Joe looks up a long second, maybe thinkin' through exactly how much time he get to be lazy afore dawn make him rise to give final rites to yesterday's cheeseburgers. He drop his head and as I ease the door shut he pops on all fours, leaps the console and shoulders the door back open.

"What?" Tat say.

"You sleepin'. Keep on, it's just Joe and me."

Tat giggle.

Maybe do all I can to keep her sleepin' in the happy land, as she's too wrought for this one. Twist 'bout and Joe's twenty yards out, nose high and sniffin' the breeze come down the hollow. Smell like crick water and the dank black earth under hemlock, back home. Damn wonderful.

Joe disappear 'round a tank-size boulder. "What you — "

I shut up on account a Tat sleepin' and trot after Joe, clued by his feet splashin' on leaves.

Droppin' a hand to the lower back I recall Ruger's under the driver seat in the tacky ass holster and Smith's in the trunk, too big to hide easy without it slidin' under foot each time I brake. And me chasin' what?

Yank, for all I know.

'Round the corner Joe's froze like a bird pointer and his voice is low.

Not three feet ahead is some kinda beast on its side, legs under a mess a rhododendron. Coat's black and shiny like coal but salted through.

Dog.

"He dead Joe?"

No. But he's not awake.

"He good people?"

He's unconscious.

"Anh... He a pit?"

Maybe some. Does that make him good?

"Nah, but he could chew off your face, give 'im cause."

On all fours I ease aside Joe and give the beast a study. He's cleaner'n Joe.

Cleaner'n me.

His throat rolls slow and deep but he don't move. Any animal what's wounded or sleepin', only play is give him room. Wisdom learned at a price.

"Tell him we're friendly, Joe."

If he talks, he heard you.

Dog don't open his eyes but he grumble. Must be goin' 'round.

"All right Yank dog, easy while I say hello. Mind yer manners... Y'all won the war and give us Leviathan. Easy now, Yank dog. I'm a friend."

Don't want to get up and over but he don't move. Knees close as I dare, arms out to bat aside snappin' teeth if they come, I stretch both hands to his coat.

And now my neck's even more sweaty as I recall Achilles' teeth 'bout my throat and the time I had to shoot a prize-fighter pit. This animal afore me ain't got the scars of a fighter.

Yank dog grumbles.

No dog want a stranger at his back, but the rhododendron won't let me in front. Maybe this feller's smart 'nough to hear a friend even if he can't see him. So, I love on his shoulder then up behint the ears.

"Yeah, puppydog... Like that, don't ya? You a good puppydog. You a good puppydog. You a good puppydog. Whoda good puppydog? Lookit the good puppydog, Joe."

You know that annoys the shit out of us, right?

"Yeah puppydog. Yes you are. Yes you are."

Hey buddy, come on. No shit. What's going on? You need some help?

I stop rubbin' his ear and listen.

Nothin'.

"Guess he ain't a talker, Joe-sy Wales."

Yes he is. He's just about to give out.

"Don't look injured but the ribs show. and he don't breathe too deep."

What's that up there? Yellow?

"Rope?"

His feet are tied.

CHAPTER THREE

"Easy, Yank dog. Easy. I got to move 'round here a bit, 'right? Easy."

I shift back and right, pass in front his face and give as much space as the rhododendron permit.

"That's right. Let's get a look here."

Both front legs is tied together and both back, bound at the ankle and coiled half up the legs.

What kind of mother—

"Only one kind, Joe. Only one kind." Movin' slow I say, "Aright, Yank dog. Let me do my work. Nice 'n easy."

Who's the good puppydog?

"That's right, Joe. Lookit the good puppydog."

Some demon jackass wound half inch propylene rope on an old dog's legs, spun ten times and finished with a... looks like a granny knot with six half-hitches. Idiot.

Asshole.

I shoulder crawl under waxy green leaves. Work his front

toes while Yank dog growl, then try and push the tag back in under the last loop but the knot's cinched tight. We need some blood in them feet. I fetch my Leatherman blade and cut.

Joe lay in front Yank dog's head and commiserates.

I get his feet free and since I can't sit up, lay sidewise and work a paw in each hand, pump out the old blood. Dog feet is most always cold, so no tellin' the damage. I ain't slept all night but even if I had I don't know as I could tolerate the moment any better. They's some cruel ass people out there no matter where a fella roam.

We got you now. Hang in there.

Yank dog lift his head a half inch and growl.

I retreat 'round the way I come and scoop him under the shoulder and hip. His jaw snap at my face but his head's a foot from mine. Teeth sound soft as wood blocks.

"Easy, now."

I lift him clear and once I get my knees figured, stand one leg at a time.

"Okay Joe, let's bring him home."

Come 'round the rock and see the Eldorado passenger door 's open. Closer still. Tat's bare legs is showing' beneath.

We get close enough the rustlin' leaves draw her head to the window. She pop up behind the door wigglin' up her drawers and her stomach don't show nothin' yet. But I see the way these women do it, one day she's rails and the next she got knockers like softballs. Keep a feller distracted while Fate change its name to Doom.

Tat say, "What is that?"

"Yankee puppy dog. Someone left him tied."

"He doesn't have a collar."

"Tied his legs so he couldn't move."

Her mouth parts. She close her eyes. "Sick."

Yank dog's gettin' heavy. I bet someone mix the pit with some mastiff, couple generations back.

Tat put her face in his and I rotate him back.

"What can I do?" she say.

"Don't let him chew your face. Let's get him some blankets from the back seat."

"How about some water from Joe's dish?"

"Even better."

She folds blankets thick and situates 'em on the ground and while I work back down to the knees and rest Yank dog on his side agin, Tat fetch a bowl of water and yesterday's stash of cheeseburgers.

"Them good yet?"

"Maybe grab a quarter pounder out the bag and set it on the engine block. He'll need a few minute to steady himself anyway."

Yank dog lift his head like his master was familiar with the quarter pounder. Now I think on it, I do like a pickle in the morning, and maybe the bun might soak some the coffee I drunk all night.

"Maybe put three burgers on the block, 'right?"

Tat smiles, first time since she kill three men. Says she, "Don't you want any?"

"Better make 'em all."

Put the mind back on the dog. He got the black coat with old dog white. Gray whiskers and brows, eyes you don't know if they's just old or old 'n sad. He seen some devils in his day.

Door close. Hood latch release.

Joe sit up. Slop his tongue 'cross the jowl.

Yank dog drop his head flat on the blankets. He ain't shift

his legs since I loose 'em. Stretched aside him I work the toes like afore, flex the joints a little. He let me, but a dead dog'd let me too. If he don't get curious at the quarter pounder, I dunno.

Might have to do somethin' I won't like.

"How long?" Tat say.

"Close the hood and give 'em a half hour."

"Where are you going?"

I'm on my feet pattin' pockets. Smith. Knew I was missin' something. Open the driver door and release the trunk.

"You think he needs gold?" Tat say.

Ladyfolk get moods sometimes, is all.

Clouds roll in quick and they's no tellin' if it's rain or hail 'til an ice ball knock your eye out.

"Pistol. I'm gonna walk up the hill. See the lay."

"Is that smart? To have a pistol that size on your leg?"

"Why not?"

"Because people will think you are looking for a fight."

I look at Yank dog.

"I am."

"Well don't. Take the small one. The Ruger. Then no one knows you're trouble until you want him to know."

It's been six gallon of coffee and six half cooked burgers since I brush my teeth. Mouth got a funk and now Tat's savin' my life. Mostly dead dog and no answers. Thank you, Lord, I'll have two.

"Seriously, Baer. You have to think about your obligations."

"What's that mean?"

"It means I don't want to raise your baby without you, and you don't have a care in all the world."

"On account I prefer a .44?"

"On account you only think of yourself."

"Well…"

Clamp the right hand on top the door and just 'bout to slam it I think on Yank dog and my manners.

"Joe, I'm takin' a walk. You in charge."

I grab Smith out the trunk and stride off with holster floppin' 'til I get the belt about me and fastened. Round the boulder where we found Yank dog, and I keep on a hundred feet afore the land begin to climb. Hear the tractor trailers from the interstate we pass last night afore the exit. Woman tell a man what gun to carry?

Tomorrow it'll be which socks. Wear the fuckin' argyles. And I'll be, Argyle?

And she'll say, Look it up in your Funk and Wagnalls.

I know what a fuckin' argyle is.

Though it's only on account the song, and them fellers had it right. Grab that woman by the hair and lookit that cave man go.

Hill's too steep for mental musin' and now I get about a bit, the mornin' bowels want to graduate a couple seniors. At a young hemlock I drop the drawers and wiggle in the low branches and after a couple stab wounds to the backside I squat and at the keenest moment discover a pad of cool thick moss on the side of a quartzy sandstone. I peel it off squattin' and press the tender green to my cheek. Close the eyes 'til the smell of somethin' wicked this way comes.

Woman's with child and I'm fifty-three.

Moss is knit good and don't crumble at the crucial moment, and I don't know if it's this draw in particular or all Pennsylvania got it, but that's superior wipin' moss over what I grew up on in Gleason.

Tell me which gun to carry. Not a year ago she couldn't shoot a water pistol and now she gonna —

Bite the tongue. Got to mind the thoughts as Mags say, as thoughts is things. Build up in the brain like crud and one day I want to love on Tat and won't be able on account the knurled up angry memories. It's in the fuckin' physics.

Plus, I got too much coffee sloppin' about the mind. Got the wheels spinnin' and won't grab. How the hell 'm I gonna raise a boy on the lam?

Least it's possible.

Tat drop a girl I'll shoot myself. Only thing decent.

On top the hill it's wood left and right and highway in front. Head west where the ground's high and clear. Climb the deer fence and walk the tall grass. Lotta Budweiser Indians left artifacts. Coors too. Looks like a toddler's tank top tangled in the weeds. I fetch and hold it at the shoulders. No rips nor tears. Boil it a good half hour it'll be clean as what come off the store shelf. I tuck it in the pocket.

Chuck it. My boy gets new.

No traffic a good quarter mile; I scoot across the highway and over the other guardrail. See if I can get up the next bank 'fore the cars come.

Nope.

Like climbin' a twelve pitch roof covered in thatch and mornin' dew.

Now the cars is honkin'. I take another look; none got lights on the roof. Cut my angle and take the hill at a slant.

Up top I gander. Behind where I come from is woods 'til the land roll over.

But ahead is more hill.

I slip 'n slide down the other side and when the traffic

breaks, skitter 'cross and climb the guardrail. Not so long ago I'd a jumped it. Now I'm fifty-three. Mercy.

The crick leads right back to camp. I get down on the rocks and hell if they ain't a man size tunnel under the highway. Water backed up a bit on the other end, but I tuck away the information like an old man keeps hubcaps.

Ain't time to head back so I turn 'bout and follow the crick into the wood. Trees all hemlock, tall with the low branches dead or long ago knocked off so the bottom fifteen feet of forest is nothin' but trunks and rocks and slope. Mossy boulders. This year's pinecones and last. Air smell fresh enough to strip bare and bathe in it.

But I'm far too old for such frivolication. Got a near dead dog needs justice and Tat's knocked up too.

Stop in my tracks and wince.

I left Tat cussin' and the trunk wide open. Keys on the seat and gold in the bucket.

Reckon I'll know her mind when I get back.

For now, they's land to see. The crick path wiggle a good four five feet lower'n the terrain. Sizable stone in the water and I wonder what my mother'd say if I told her these was Ice Age rocks. It's an easy slip of the mind, wade into beyond and say *Hello Ma, been a while*. I stand and let the eyesight haze out and once the center of my forehead float a little I recall my mother and dream her present, so I don't know what part of the concoction's past or future. But the morning breeze's fresh and homey. Air bubble up out the Appalachian earth is richer 'n the air out West. Most of dirt is dead plants and animals. Bugs and rabbit shit. Lotta deer shit too. Once all that livin' matter rots the stink out, in North Carolina you can scoop up a taste and it'll be sweet and cool in the mouth, 'specially in the spring. I get on my knees real quick still thinkin' of Ma in the opaline shimmer, so pretty and young it's like she's new, and just like that time she showed me what good North Carolina dirt taste like, I claw a handful and taste Pennsylvania.

Spit that shit out and dust off my knees. Cough.

This fuckin' place ain't right.

CHAPTER FOUR

I keep on the crick path 'til on the left it open to a road with a natural gas well at the end and beyond, a field up the hill to a crown of trees and the horizon beyond. Sky look crisp like a fella could rip off half and hear it crunch like cabbage. Hills got layers, waves. False summits. Maybe a mile to the tree covered dome.

Back the way I come it's interstate, woods and the sound of tire on cement. Ahead, it's like the sour taste in my mouth color the view, so it ain't the blue sky and green leaves put me in a mood, but the Pennsylvania dirt I keep toothin' off the tongue.

I dunno. Need a think.

Even in Gleason with a whole town of liars, only the air had a pink glow, and that emanate from the houses. They's no juice nor red out here, and if I ain't taste the land and see the dog with its legs tied I wouldn't know they was so much evil in these parts. 'Cept the history, accourse. Abe Lincoln sayin' we'll kill you free fuckers to keep you in the Union, so the verbs on the lips of a hundred million folk change from the United States are to the United States is. That tyranny of industry and bankers is all 'round the North, and a fella tuned to history can see it in the little things.

Blue collar man in the North look like his ailments been treated with more and more leeches. A good bleedin'll solve everything, thinks the tycoon, so he take more and more lifeblood as his own.

I agree, sometimes, on the utility of a good bleedin'.

But aside from the history, they's somethin' uncanny wicked hereabouts.

Part of me want to pull the thread and see how much hit the ground afore the veil falls and the naked unglorious truth stand lookin' back.

Somewhere in these woods or fields or houses is a locus.

Maybe that ain't the word. Maybe a hive. Sure as I taste it I can feel it too. No juice, just the force behind it. Like afore the mouth goes open, they's an untold lie, sittin' on the tongue.

I walk.

Pass the gas well, still got the pulverized rock all 'round from when they drill it. Tree trunks upturned at the lot edge, giant tire tracks like they was makin' monster bricks and left 'em in the mud where they stamp 'em.

This well is new.

Twenty-foot pond with algae and no fish. Cattails. Water's been still so long it got that toxic sheen: film on top, broth below. Like lookin' through glass to a dark room where poison air kill whatever lived inside.

Standin' at the water's edge I turn a circle, fade out the

highway noise and tune to a wisp of breeze, enough to launch a couple leaves lopin' after each other in a fat swirl of wind.

I keep after the hill. With a hundred yards' elevation the cleared farmland's like a V with wood on each side and a hill at the top. I mind the field and keep the wood all 'round so I don't stomp some feller's crops and after a good fifteen minute I'm on top the dome and my lungs is happy enough to quit.

Below's a pond, mebbe a lake. Hillside and beyond glows with morning light. They's a burned barn and a shitty old house still standin'. Row of trees and another barn and house, lookin' good. Perfect siding, new cement driveway.

Never woulda suspected a lake. Funny I didn't smell it. Look to be a mile long and a couple hundred yard wide at the skinny point near the bend. Maybe it's ten mile and not one. Can't see if it's a dammed up crick or natural. Off 'n the right's a pair of farms sit too close one another. Just like I saw after my house burnt in Gleason and after Brown's house burnt in-after, they's a stone foundation with a charred shipwreck inside, black timbers juttin' like afore the barn burned it pirated gold and women and spoils off the high seas.

Or maybe this lake.

Try and look away but that clusterfuck spectacle kinda pull the eye.

Don't look like a workin' farm when it burned.

Grass growed up tall. Chicken coop's roof fell in. Even the shed's rotted gray, missin' side boards, half the door off the tracks.

Maybe these people rent the fields to some other operation still earnin' lives out the land.

Curious how them barns come about so close. Fella from

the first could stand on his roof and spin a cow pie at the other, and that's closer'n regular country folk find comfortable.

Yanks? Who knows?

These farms ain't the same operation; least they wasn't at the start. See how the one use that skinny strip of woods like a fence? It's like each clan lay claim to the last stretch of lake... though no one want any the rest, far's the eye can see.

So up here in Yank country they bind an old dog's legs and leave him to die. The best dirt taste like shit rolled in bear grease and the farms get planted back to back, and once they feed a generation or two is left to rot.

Maybe if I wasn't prejudiced agin everything north of Virginny, I wouldn't see it this way. The fields and forest is beautiful and the water reflect light in a million tiny glitters. On the left at water's edge, a pontoon's moored to a tree with yellow rope. And up above the land become fields of corn and wheat and the hills roll into pretty skies.

They's a road next the lake and lookin' back the way I come, I maybe coulda found it and got here faster.

I keep next the trees so I don't draw eyes, and since I been awake all night and got a bit of news ain't settled in yet, I brace a tree and fold the knees. Skooch out the heels and plop my ass on a stump.

Tat's got my baby in her belly and on the whole I wish I was more in love with life'n I am. Older I get, the keener my understanding grows of just how rotten one man can be to another. Spent most my life just watchin', hidin' out best I could. Too many lies to count, let alone combat.

But now I got a bun in Tat's oven, and that poor boy's 'bout to join a world that'll do its ugly best to make him a slave to modern stupidities.

Shoulda kept my dick in my drawers.

I'll not marry Tat. They's no one to wed us and God Almighty don't need the witness if we don't. But that baby in her belly's mine.

Splinters in the ass from where the chain sawed cuts didn't quite meet in the middle afore the tree snap and fell. Shift. Pucker.

I don't know the number of my days, but what days I got'll be renderin' a small plot worthy of my child's innocence.

In the old times a farmer didn't homestead all the land he could see, as he knew he couldn't till it. So he grab a patch and say this'll sustain us. This we'll keep safe as ours, and if the bad men ride in, this is where we'll cut 'em down.

This is the hill we live on, so this is the hill we die on, if need be.

I can't murder all the evil what's out there. But 'tween now and the time my boy sets himself loose on the world, them eighteen years is my plot of land, and I'll be with Tat the whole time, and I'll raise that boy to do right. I don't got to kill all the evil out there, just what evil seeks to interfere with raisin' my boy.

I'll bring him up to do right. Stand so tall, he'll walk over trees to scratch his nuts.

Need a good long nap. Food. Drink.

They's evil here, I can feel it. But they's evil elsewhere too, and I don't seem to know sometimes 'til it clock me in the laundry room.

This is where we stay.

CHAPTER FIVE

Smell bacon afore the smoke. Belly feels empty and I ain't walked two mile. Gettin' decrepit. The old wounds is healed, much as they heal any more. But usetacould walk all day on a fifth of shine, better'n half a week on a jug. Long as I had some cabbage for roughage, keep shit movin' inside.

Now it take a good half mile to lube the joints and two mile the big pipe.

Knew my whole life the day was comin'. The day ain't arrived, but I'm hearin' more and more whispers sayin', dust to dust.

Once I'm at the flat at the bottom of the hill, come up on camp and Stinky Joe trot out from behind the Eldorado and meet me.

Give him a pat.

Yank dog's layin' on a blanket bed next a small fire with a greasy pan and no bacon. His eyeballs find me and his brow dips like he knows all human hell is comin' for him. Tell me somethin' 'bout who he live with afore.

"How you feelin', Yank dog? If you got all that bacon down yer gullet, you wasn't too bad off to begin with."

"Most of it is in a jar," Tat say. "He ate a piece, though."

Tat sit on a flat rock she musta drug from the crick, along with the rocks 'round the fire. She's real close the FOR SALE sign and it'd be a shame if something happen to it. So, I give it a tug, push it sideways, wiggle it a bit and quit. Steel post is in the ground good enough to satisfy itself and so I'm satisfied too.

Tat go the car and come back with bread buns and a jar of bacon. I grab a bun, kneel at the fire.

"You can put that meat away," says I. "And thank you."

Dip that bread in grease and give Yank dog a sniff. He flick his tongue, lay his head back on the ground.

"Hungry? Want some? This'll put hair on your chest. Yessir. Lookit that good puppydog. Who's a good puppydog?"

Oh fuckin' A.

"You think he's had too much lovin' in his life, Joe? That it?"

Joe shake his head.

Words mean things, Baer. He isn't a puppydog. He's a person.

"I know that."

You better.

Stinky Joe look away and step a few feet. Gimme another look and head toss. I chew off the bun and follow Joe out of Yank dog's earshot, down by the crick.

His name is Carpenter.

"Uhn."

That's all he said.

"Nothin' else?"

That's all he said.

"You said that."

What else do you want?

"I'm just surprised sometimes you talk at all."

This conversation? Now you're wondering why the dog talks?

"No, not exactly. No. Can't a man enjoy a little bemusement, if it don't harm nobody? How the fuck is it that every fuckin' time I open my mouth I got someone or 'nother pissed?"

I'm not pissed.

"I didn't say you was."

There's only one other someone.

"You sayin' she's pissed?"

As much as you are.

"Good."

Okay.

"And that Yank dog. Carpenter. Don't push him too much for information. His estimate of my kind ain't the best. Fact, it's dead on the money. So, it'll take him seein' somethin' different 'til he believe somethin' different. I got some ideas to work on and we got time to let him come 'round. Is all."

Stinky Joe step in front so I got to stop. Send me lurchin'.

"What?"

What if he doesn't live that long?

"Then he'll be floatin' in the nonlocal. You heard me say all this a couple dozen times by now. He'll see the light. He'll go through the tunnel. He'll spot his ma and pa and they'll all sniff each other's asses. You know all this."

Joe shakin' his head, got a bit of a spark in his eye.

We're doing something about this, right? We're going to find the son of a bitch?

"We're gonna do somethin', Joe. We're *damn* sure gonna do somethin'. Out my way. I got work to do."

I push off and he scoots.

Eat more bread but it ain't got the grease. Now I need water. I head back to the crick and kneelin' at a mossy rock under a hemlock, spot a green tricycle about two feet down in the water pooled afore headin' through the six-foot pipe under the road.

Guess that's par for the course in these United States.

I wonder if the Almighty'll ever make litterin' a capital offense, such as to send a Destroyer like me after the garbage chuckers.

Or maybe that's only a crime in the world to come.

Head back the Eldorado and swig Turkey 'til the throat's clear and the bacon grease beckons. Another dip, this time landin' a good dollop on top. I bite and talk while I chew:

"Hey there, legs. You got that device? Bring up a map?"

Tat fetch her phone and I finish breakfast and lunch. She tap the screen and hold it at me.

I look. Check the sun. Orient the map in my skull and point.

"I'm headed thataway."

"What's that - a - way?"

"Over there."

"Asshole. What is over there?"

Laugh. It feels good and necessary sometimes, in the thick of livin'.

"Reynoldsville, accordin' to that map."

"Why are you going there? You haven't slept since yesterday."

"Not strictly true. I caught a couple winks drivin' through Ohio."

Tat ain't impressed.

"Say, your tits is bigger. Right?"

Huff, spin, stomp.

"Hey! Ain't they?"

She struts fifteen feet and stares lookin' into hemlock.

"This is important!" Grin at her back and her ass got a new plump to it, too. "Thataway," says I, walkin' off. "Be back afore dark. Joseph, you mind your ma."

I want to come with you. Make plans.

"Nope. We got a guest and Tat's got a ball of Moxie in her belly. You're on guard."

Joe stop walkin'.

"I mean that," says I. "On guard! It's why we hairy types get the privilege of ownin' testicles and a sack to carry 'em in."

Joe connects eyes with me and I see the words hit him. He does a tiny nod with a squint and that tell me he'll die to protect that woman and my son, if he got to.

"I appreciate ya."

I head for the road I spot from the hilltop, woulda made my first walk around easier. It's hill and left turn and still more hill. Then the interstate pass over, then fields left and right. Ahead, though not yet in view, is the two houses I saw a bit ago, one with the burned barn.

Can't help it but the place has a draw on me. Down in the hollow where I left Tat and crew, they's Ice Age rocks like Ma said we didn't have in North Carolina, and I knew we did. I like how the crick come through. Go upstream a few hundred yards and the water'd be fine for boilin'. The air smell of hemlock and the dirt's black and rich. Any land not paved for travel is green with somethin'.

I could see a homestead, if the Almighty was to spare me runnin' across folks needin' sent forward. A couple year off-duty, make sure the boy gets to be number one when it matters most. And if I was gonna be here a year or five, I bet a gold coin I could find a place up there in the hollow to set a still and hide the smoke. Mebbe get a truck like I had — or no, since I'm walkin' and got time to give the muse full consideration, I'll take a 1965 International D1100, and the girl was sittin' on the bed at the county fair when I first felt the scrotal roll and sensed somethin' 'bout the other kind of human being had the potential to amuse me.

Stand on the roadside lookin' at a telephone line, like it might write her name for me, since I can't recall.

Cindy Wasson.

She toss a smile 'bout knock me sideways. And she was narrow in the eyes like she was *lookin'*. Dreamed on that girl every night for three years 'til Ruth come along and give me carnal progress.

Damn.

Damn!

Look at the old pervert standin' on the roadside, seein' girls in the clouds.

But truth is I wasn't lustin' after the girl, just bein' young enough to make pokin' her right agin.

And Tat ain't but a year older'n that.

If a man knew what he'd become, he'd fight harder for everything worth fightin' for.

Keep walkin' to a T and go left, as that's the way to town.

It'd be a couple mile as the crow flies. Three four on these roads.

Breeze carry some humidity off the lake and I think on that, how a still next a lake could be a good thing. Boil mash as the breeze take the stink over the water. Anyone smelled it, and didn't know what he was smellin', might suspect the water's rank.

The first of the two houses come in view, though it's the one farthest off. Other's hid by wood. Bunch of election signs at the driveway. In a quarter mile I see past the signs — more middle fingers in support of Levi Hardgrave — back the drive to the charred barn. Air off the lake beyond carry the wet smell of burned wood, then the whiff is gone. The house sittin' next the barn is old as anything you ever see. Couple trees in front, dead and need cut down. Prob'ly got critters livin' under the porch, the trees is so thick and so close.

Some us country folk is idiots. We acknowledge that.

The other house ain't as old and the folks stayin' there now got money. Lawn looks like they took it to the barber for a trim, everythin' so neat and perfect. Snip snip. On the approach as I get aperture 'round the garage, I behold a sight that'd surely set Chicago Mags' mouth a flappin'.

Someone'd need to explain how this moment could happen, and only someone versed in cosmic fuckery and voodoo, and of course the higher religions and quantum physics, would be qualified to hazard a hypothesis on how they's a 1965 International D1100 pickup truck on the lawn for sale, like I dreamed it on that very lawn.

CHAPTER SIX

That truck wasn't there a hour ago when I did my walk.

I pick up my pace and the ache heats up where the punji stick got me. Them fuckin' Graves people.

The International's painted black and buffed so the clouds in the sky roll 'cross the paint. It's sittin' there real enough I bet I could pinch myself and it'll still be there.

So I do, and it is.

One of the mystical things Chicago Mags said I'd see, now I got connections and favor.

If I could only manifest Cindy Wasson too.

Except older, as I ain't a pervert.

Her daddy's International was stripped down to a wood flat bed and one time he drove with Cindy and me on the back out pickin' mushrooms, halfway down the hill to Old Fort where the fire left so many acres perfect for 'em. Goin' downhill we brace agin the front, no trouble. But climbin' the hill on them rutted and rocky forest roads, she and me 'bout bounce our asses out the truck, 'til we each flip over and sprawl out, legs spread and fingers draggin'.

One them bounces landed me square on my kickstand and I didn't care if I fell off or not.

This International's got a For Sale sign in the window and a phone number. I bet a knock on the door'd work as well. Get close the paint and it's clear and perfect. Glass is polished with a rag this mornin', it looks so happy. And inside the truck is black leather seats.

Fuck.

Ain't original.

Got a radio inside, black, modern, with all the buttons. Speakers like to have a rock concert on the front seat.

Still, a fine lookin' machine.

Get on all fours and dip to the front bumper. Roll to my back and squiggle a few inch in under, lookin' oil or anything else. But these people with the perfect lawn is also the sorta people that wash the fuckin' underside they vehicles, so I can't tell shit 'bout the maintenance.

But stands to reason if they wash the underside they's like to change the oil when it needs.

Time to see how much they lie.

Regain my feet and hear the front door. Start movin' that-away. More commotion. I look and it's a woman joined a man. He got one arm high and she got both raised between, and I get the feelin' it's a race to see which is gonna talk at me first.

Now I'm lookin' that way, I see a big red, white and blue sign on the lawn in front the house.

Re-Elect Wolfgang A McClellan
U.S. House of Representatives.

"Hello," the woman say. "Before my husband helps you with the truck, have you been walking this way from the highway? Have you seen an old black dog, anywhere?"

"This gentleman didn't come to talk about a dog. He's interested in this fine American Classic automobile, manufactured in 1965."

He's a big grin sittin' under gray hair with Brylcreem furrows I spot from thirty feet. Button up short-sleeve shirt, tight at the shoulder.

"What's to keep you from driving her home today?" says he, coming' down the steps.

Magnificent. A car salesman happen to live in the house with a truck for sale on the lawn.

"Mister?" the woman says.

The old man point to the door and she go to it.

"I prob'ly will drive it home today, if I want."

"That so? You carrying twenty thousand on you, cash? Because we don't take checks around here."

"I wouldn't trust cash as far as I could burn it. I got gold."

"Twenty grand in gold?"

"Ninety-nine point infinity pure Canadian Maple Leafs. But you just advanced the conversation well beyond where it deserve to be. I don't hear this truck runnin' yet, and I don't see under the hood."

"I can remedy that."

"You was a car salesman, right? Pretty good at it?"

"I was. Long time ago."

"Well, that's fine as water. Cars gotta sell, right? You got the keys for this thing?"

"You carryin' your drivers' license?"

"Old habits, huh?"

"That's right. I'll need to hold your drivers' license, before we take it for a drive."

"Accourse. Which I'll provide once I hear the engine run and get my look under the hood."

He study me a long ten second and I hold his eye like behind mine is brick and he dip his head. I won't have no trouble out him no more, and it'll just be two men sharin' the same respect back and forth. That's the way it's s'pose to work.

"That'll do, neighbor. What's your name?"

Fuck. This agin.

"Alden Boone."

"Well Alden, it's a pleasure to meet you." He throw his hand and I shake it. "I'm Silas. Silas McClellan. All this land you see most of the way to town used to be McClellan land. We were the original settlers and we have traditions."

"You sure can sell."

He grin, tight, then add a sparkle to the eye — he know he's fulla shit. Jolly good fellow.

I don't like him.

"Now this International D Eleven Hundred's been in our family since I bought it in 1966. We used it for years as a regular work truck, out in the fields and all over. And you know how things progress, you see new models... In fact, I bought an F-150 to replace this one and put it in the shed. All this time passes, I get promoted, things are going well and I forget about the truck. Oh, I know it's there, I suppose. I just don't ever want to do anything with it. Well anyhow, wait 'til you retire. What do you do for a living, Alden?"

"Uh-huh. Go on."

"Your line of work?"

"Oh, I'm independently wealthy. Thank you."

"You are?"

"Havin' a lotta gold'll do that."

"I see. So, the truck was in the shed over there until after I retired, when it started calling out to my heart, almost, telling me there was still time to do something worthwhile with what life I have left, you know?"

"This a long story? Does the engine run?"

"Straight to the point. I understand."

The man opens the door. Silas, he said. He grab the roof and navigate inside the truck, and I watch how his body go slow, like he's afraid the sinew might snap. Dust to dust.

Silas hold the key in the air with significance I fail to grok, then he make dramatic faces at me while he stick it in and start the truck. I look away. This man enjoy the show too much.

"Look at this!" says Silas. He reach to the glove box and come back with his hand holdin' a small tablet. "Look at this. I kept a log of every mile. Every single mile this truck drove. You don't see that."

"You don't see that," says I. "Step on the gas a little, let me hear you hold it steady, just above the idle."

"The engine isn't warm, yet. No matter, you hear how smooth that is?"

Sparks and a flash of red. But I wouldn't a needed the curse to tell me, as I looked 'cross this place from the far hill and the truck wasn't here. Meanin' he drove it from the garage on the other side of the house, at a minimum.

"It's warm enough from you drivin' it out, not ten minutes back. Or you forget?"

"I forget."

Silas step out the vehicle and lift the hood. While I look, he get back in the truck and start steppin' on the gas.

"You've never seen a better-cared-for vehicle in your life," says Silas.

I fetch my wallet and the card with Alden Boone and my image. Drop the hood and give Silas the license.

"Slide over if you want to sell this thing."

I open the door and his head bob don't last a half bounce afore he liven up and skoot. I hop in. Press the clutch and get the feel of the shifter.

"That's real easy. You work some grease in this mornin', didn't you?"

I give the gas pedal some pressure and shift the clutch. Spin the wheel and the ratio's higher'n I'da thought, but I never drove the International. Transmission engage smooth and though the truck don't got the same balls 's the Eldorado, the engine respond without hesitation.

I get on the road and head away from where I come. Truck rides stiff, after the Cadillac. Seems to fit my new frame of mind, now I got Moxie on the way.

Tat don't know I give him a name, yet.

"Clear title? It ain't salvage or anything. No horse shit."

"No horse shit," Silas say, and I don't get a spark or nothin'.

"All right," says I. "Gold's at nine hundred per. I'll give you twenty ounce."

"That leaves me two grand short. Twenty-three."

"Twenty-one."

"Twenty-two."

"Sounds good. So, you got a politician in the family?"

He smile big.

"That's my son. I couldn't be prouder. This country needs reform! We can all agree on that. Don't get me started."

"I won't. Scout's honor."

"Wolfgang's about to win his third term."

"Sure thing?"

"He's running unopposed."

"That so."

"You saw the neighbor's place, right? The barn that burned?"

"Uh-huh." I brake and take a driveway. Turn around. Salesman can't stop runnin' his trap.

"That barn you saw is the reason Wolfgang is running unopposed. After watching my son serve our country for two terms, our neighbor decides to run against him. For Congress. We're in the country. Regular people. What kind of neighbor runs for national elected office to keep up with the Joneses?"

"And you burn his barn?"

"What? No! Of course not. He did — proven insurance fraud. His campaign was broke. Can you believe that?"

"Not everyone can sell shit good as you, Silas."

"I know. And the stupidity of the common man is what pisses me off — no offense of course."

"I'd hafta be common or stupid to find it."

I brake hard and he stop himself from the windshield with his arms. Cut the wheel. Park at his house.

Silas nod at the burned barn.

"What was stupid was that the feud was over. We treated

the Hardgraves like regular people growing up. Bah. It's a long story and you want to buy a fine American-made truck."

"You make a good point."

I exit the vehicle.

He climb out the other side.

"Title's in the house. You have your, uh, gold on your person?"

Nod.

"I'll be right back."

He step to the house and I go 'round the truck, seein' each detail. Open the other door and close it. Drop the tailgate. Jump on the bed a couple time, over each wheel. Look under the hood agin, check the belts and hoses. I wouldn't be led astray by the nonlocal anyway, so me lookin' over the vehicle's all for show.

He come out with paper in hand and I pull coin from my belt. Twenty-two leave me feelin' light but I got fiat for the groceries.

We transact on the truck bed, he sign the title and I stack the coins in fives. He put one to his teeth.

"Don't lie. You wouldn't know if that was white metal."

"I'd know if it was white."

"But not without lookin'."

"But I'd look."

"That you would, Silas."

"The challenger — what I was saying earlier about my son's election. Look at these signs, giving people the middle finger sign. Like that's going to work. Anyway, my son's challenger committed suicide — that's his house over there. His name was Levi Hardgrave. The Feds busted him for insurance fraud, and he committed suicide. That's why my son is running unopposed."

I blink.

"The Feds?"

"Be sure and vote on election day," Silas says.

"Tell you a secret," says I. "You don't want my view on the politics."

"Every vote matters."

I get inside my truck, fire the engine.

"Say, that dog your wife was askin' about…"

"Yeah?"

"Was that her animal? She the one to look after him?"

"Why?"

"I found him close to dead in the woods."

"Oh. God. Why didn't you mention it earlier?"

"Like you said. I stop in to buy a truck."

"Yes, she looked after him. It's my son's dog but she looked after him whenever Wolfgang was in DC."

"Washington."

"Right. DC. This last time, the dog just disappeared — the dog's name is Carpenter. She was saying earlier that Carpenter hadn't been around since Wolfgang flew back to Washington, like the dog knew something, you know? He's an old dog. She thought he might have wandered off in the woods. You understand."

Silas' eyes is red.

"The congressman in the house? Love to get a word with him."

"No, I just said he flew back to Washington."

"So maybe don't tell your lady 'bout the dog. Sound like the news'd break her heart."

I press the gas pedal. Turn. Hold my arm from wavin', as I reserve the right to disenjoy assholes.

"Hey," says Silas.

Brake.

"Yeah?"

"You mind taking care of the dog? You know. Just deal with him for us. I'd take it as a special favor, if you spared my wife and I the upset."

I get the current on both arms and got to look away from his glowin' eyes.

I drive, and wonder how this man's lies fit the whole.

CHAPTER SEVEN

LOTTA FOLKS SHOWIN' THEM RAISED MIDDLE FINGER SIGNS. That Hardgrave fella's popular.

Near every house 'long the route has a salute flyin' high. Does the heart good. Drive the roads from the map I recall to Reynoldsville, and after wavin' two three times to folk expectin' to see a different face behint the wheel of a truck that's hard to not see, I realize I bought the wrong vehicle for avoidin' the notice of the people.

But they's no need they ever connect my face to any man from North Carolina. Been a bit since I saw my mug on a newspaper or hotel television screen. I keep the shave tight and the hair lookin' like a banker and no one ever imagine me smart 'nough to be a hillbilly.

Keep talkin' myself into thinkin' I could stay in these parts a while, is all.

I see the land's promise. The brightness of the sun and the beauty of the hills. I'll never be safe visitin' Gleason agin, and though I ain't heartsick over it, if I was I'd be less so, on account how west Pennsylvania's just as soggy green as where I come from.

Plus the Amish is good people, what I hear. They don't do any of the fun stuff, but none of the pure ass rotten, neither. Rippin' good deal in a neighbor.

And soon as I think it, I spot another one of these confessed idiots we country folk all acknowledge. Trailer parked on a side hill, lawn of tall grass and a couple junkers in the thicket beyond. Use to be a row of pines in front, but this fella cut 'em off leavin' stumps eight foot high. On top each stump is a sizable rock, ten twelve inch. Each stone's painted solid: red, white or blue.

Take that shit in a minute and try to grok what the hell the fella's tryin' to say, and it hit me them colors mean somethin', though different things to different folk. The minute in confusion wasn't the colors of the flag but what the hell he mean leavin' eight-foot stumps with painted rocks on top.

But as I keep on to town and think on the bigger principles, that fella with the painted rocks come 'cross in a different light.

A man leave eight-foot stumps and painted rocks next the road, that's a statement. Since he could cut the nonsense down but don't, he's content he's sayin' what he want to say. He's proud of them stumps, and though the tut-tut women like to cluck pride comes afore the fall, a man *without* a dose of pride in somethin' ain't worth a shit at nothin'.

Keep an eye on the fella with no pride, as he got no character.

It's easy 'nough to have pride, after all. Only thing a fella need is to think he's done somethin' good. And it don't matter how good, on account he sets the scale. He could be satisfied with a two-inch turd if he want. Point bein', it don't matter how good he actually is, only that he *wants to be good* — enough to choose seein' himself that way. The holy people'll say every man's a sinner, and the foundation of the Christian moral sense ain't that a man is good, but that knowin' he ain't, he yet wants to be.

That's the highest hill these legs made of dirt and God-spit'll let him mount.

Since the good never happen this world, it's 'nough to want it. And the Almighty set it thataway so a man's inevitable failure breaks his heart and his humbleness splits him wide open.

Point is, pride shows a man wants to be good.

A fella that can't muster a sense a pride in something don't *want* good, is the true point, and that's the sorta prick leaves a dog tied in the woods.

So if this fella with the painted rocks don't take pride in his camper on the sidehill, or the tender love he show his lawn, I'm satisfied he'll find it in his stump monument.

Head 'cross a flat and turn left as town thickens 'round.

Go through a light and turn at the next. Park at the grocery and sit a minute in my brand new 1965 dream truck. I close my eyes and hear the engine tick. Smell the interior, not new, not old, just all its own.

Somewhere deep in the eternal, out there in the nothin', the I AM show me favor.

I am grateful.

CHAPTER EIGHT

I fill a cart with all the stuff I been thinkin' a woman oughta be able to cook her man, if she want to keep him. Enchiladas is good and all, but I'm thinkin' real appetite-stirrin' grub. Baked bread, salty butter and pot pie. Cookies with walnuts. I use to love the walnuts as a boy and it's uncanny to think of 'em so clear in the mind's eye, the taste's apparent without a boost from the imagination.

The taste just pop in the center of my mind, like the walnuts was pressed to oil, my head drilled open and the oil can give three four good squirts to the brain.

Uncanny, what a man'll think.

I'll maybe grab a bag a walnut when I spot 'em.

Tat'll need a stove and pans and all that. We'll get a trailer too, now we got a truck to drag it. Didn't look for a hitch. Have to do that. Maybe everybody with trailers keeps eight-foot stumps and colored rocks.

We'll do what we need to fit in while Tat learns to cook bread.

Humdy-de-dum.

Do-de-doe.

Does yer tits hang low?

Kidney Beans. Grab two can. Peanut butter. Okay, sure. Asparagus. Why not?

Love me some titties.

Do-de-dum.

I bought a truck!

I give each aisle full opportunity to persuade me and get the cart mostly full. Last lane is potato chips and it's been a while, so I top off on four bags of sour cream and chive.

Store's empty but for me. Town's half dead. They got one lady workin' the register and I unload on the belt. Her features is delicate 'nough I bet she smell like a flower, but her glance to my face is hollow, and her voice uninspired.

"Did you find everything?"

"I found everything, yes I did. That button on your shoulder, there."

"Yeah?"

"He the dead fella? The suicide?"

Her lapel got a button in the form of a hand with middle finger raised tall. The whole thing's blue with red and white letters and decoration, says *Levi Hardgrave for Congress!*

"He didn't commit suicide; I can guarantee that."

She got teary eyes. Hands move a little jerky.

"Oh."

"Yeah. Hey. Where are you from?" she say. "That accent?"

"Guatemala."

"Oh. Okay."

"Who's the dead man to you?"

"You aren't from around here."

"Guatemala."

"My brother."

"You still campaignin' for him."

"Of course. Half-brother. And he's going to win. We're going to fight all the way to the finish line."

"Dead."

"Exactly. And everyone will know what they did to him. It'll be obvious."

"Accourse."

"We were grassroots all the way. Look at me. Working at a grocery store. These people are so corrupt! We were pressin' the flesh. Door… to… "

She stop with a bag of extra-broad egg noodles in her hand and let the weepy moment entrench deep behind her eyeballs.

"Go ahead and take a minute, they's no one here but us."

She sniffle. Blink.

"I was his campaign manager."

"You out high school, I take it?"

"I'm thirty. I have a master's degree in marketing. The middle finger was my idea. I'm only picking up a few hours here because I needed something short term while we were campaigning. You know, until the election."

"And afterward you'd be his…?"

"Chief of Staff."

"Ah. Accourse."

"We're still going to win."

"The campaign's got real character."

"I thought of putting the middle finger on all our materials."

"Goin' over well, is it?"

"Oh, hell yeah. We were ahead in the polls, all of them." She hold my look like to bolt it down so I can't wiggle askance while she say, "Rural P-A is mad as hell. We were so far ahead the election was *over*. They had no other way to win. They murdered him."

"Lotta people resonate to the middle finger. So now what? Your dead brother win the election and the governor decide the next congress critter? You tight with the governor?"

"Pennsylvania is the crookedest state in the country. Everyone knows it."

"That's a no, on the governor."

"That's a no on all of them. We made it clear that a vote for Levi Hardgrave was like raising your middle finger to the whole establishment. See on the pin? See? Look."

She lift her pin off her boob and lean at me.

That's a hell of a nice —

"See the details of the hand? You can see the fingers are folded over, and that means you're looking at the inside of the hand, right? Now hold up your hand."

She lift my hand. Press her fingers over mine, 'cept the middle.

"See the button? It's like you're waving the middle finger yourself."

She let go my hand. Eyeball me.

"Brilliant."

"I know, right? Vote Hardgrave! It's like a big FUCK YOU to the government! We were going to change everything. That was the point."

"Man empathize. And then Levi Hardgrave didn't commit suicide."

"All that crap in the news was total lies," says she. "Pure bullshit! He did the computer searches *after* the barn burned down, and you'd be damn right if you thought there were accelerants all over. That's because they set the stupid thing on fire themselves — don't get me started. Why the hell does anybody think he was looking up accelerants? Because the police wouldn't do anything. Out there after the barn stopped smoldering, he found them! Oh, don't even! Don't even get me started."

I notice lotta Pennsylvania folk want help with restraint.

"How long ago your brother Levi, uh, not take his life?"

"Really? You just got here? You don't know any of this?"

"Got here this morning. Saw a sign for the election and that's the extent I know 'bout Walnut County. Which is otherwise charming."

"My brother was murdered three days ago. It was staged. They put the gun in his hand and left a typed suicide note. I googled the note because it looked familiar. It was the same words they used in that stupid *Save Her Bones Inside* movie. Literally— the same note. Oh, they think they're clever. This whole thing stinks and nobody'll listen because they want everything to stay crooked. Does that sum it up?"

My cart's unloaded on the belt and she's holdin' a can of Hormel chili hostage, refusin' to send it through the price scanner 'til I acknowledge her statement, eye to eye. I don't know why it matter, as I could camp twenty mile away and this town's troubles'd be removed. But like I thought earlier, this place is different. The dark has a focus: the more I travel the local parts, I feel wind formin' the funnel. Sense the whole landscape a-rotatin' like when I was a boy with the fever. I'd lay with my head steady on the pillow while the world swung loops 'round me. Walnut County's got that same disorientin' pull, and soon as I complete the thought a cloud pass over the sky and the daylight outside the grocery store window go dark, like twilight, and a thunder boom smacks like God on a gavel.

BOOM!

Just that fast, rain batters the whole town, all us, with a single-timed volley that splash up off the sidewalk like a train wreck made of water. A torrent follows and the roof is hammered chaos.

Can't help but duck, look side to side.

"I bet no one's comin' in here through all that."

She shake her head. Jaw open a little, and mute.

Nipples hard. Likes the rain.

"Hail too," says I.

Tear my eyes away and watch the downpour. A woman dash 'cross the road and leap to the sidewalk under the landin' at the bank, other side the road. She rub her head.

"I don't want my paper bags to get wet, here to the truck," says I.

She smile, thin, not yet aware the storm conspires in her favor.

"Sometimes," says I, "People's prayers get answered."

She nods. "Yeah, I don't understand."

"I didn't think you did. Sometimes I'm the one He sends to set things aright. Tell me what you know and maybe the Divine'll inspire me."

She look out the window at the rain still crashin' down. I expect Tat's good and soaked by now, if she wasn't lucky and saw it get dark first.

One more good reason to be here, as somewhere else: with all the evil locked up in one locus nearby, once I kill it the whole town'll be good to go. Seems better'n goin' someplace normal and have to deal with shit as it crop up, here, there, everywhere, turd by turd.

"Levi was my half-brother," the girl-woman say. "Same father, but his mother made him a part of the feud. He would have never had any trouble in life if she hadn't given him that awful name."

"What name?"

"Hardgrave."

"Why it awful?"

"What? You mean *after* the movie?"

"Hold on. What?"

"After the movie. You remember the movie: *Save Her Bones Inside*. Ten years ago. No — fifteen. Matthew McConiheaux. He got a Best Actor for it."

"Miss, I been outta circulation. What are we talkin' 'bout? Really?"

"Okay, you honestly don't know anything. It started with Dr. Stanley Bliesmyer. He was just a bored rich guy, a nobody, really. He wrote a book called, *Save Her Bones Inside*. I know, stupid title. It was a true-history novel, all about the feud going back to the beginning."

"I heard a that movie."

"It was all a bunch of sensationalized garbage. Trees don't talk to people."

"The feud 'tween..."

"Hardgraves and McClellans. That book — *Save Her Bones Inside* — and the moronic movie McConiheaux did based off the book — means that everyone, everywhere, thinks all Hardgraves are either cowards or psychos. And Levi wasn't even a Hardgrave. That's the kicker. And we were going to win the election despite that. That's why they freaked out."

"Who's they?"

"The establishment."

"Ah. Still fightin' The Man. And Levi Hardgrave wasn't a Hardgrave."

"No, and neither was his father. That's what Bliesmyer got wrong in the book. He's not a real scholar. He just did that thing on Hatfield and McCoy, and his publisher wanted another book real fast, you know, while they were making money. So, he came up here for two weeks and got the story of the Hardgraves and the McClellans."

Rain still comin' down hard enough it's plain the Almighty want me here inside. Don't matter. She keep talkin'.

"Because of that movie, to this day, everyone around here still thinks of two people when they hear Hardgrave and neither was any good. Oh, but Matthew won an Oscar! Asshole. And that's the thing. Angus was a McCLELLAN, his father was the grand wizard of evil, and if you ask me, that's the most interesting point in the whole stupid story. Anyone local will tell you — McConiheaux missed the main point."

"Still a fine actor. Uh-huh. Ain't he?"

"And Levi just got stuck with the Hardgrave name because his mother kept her married name when she was single again and got knocked up at Woodstock. That's the truth."

"I'll take it on your say so."

"They say the land itself is cursed up by the lake. The history tells you that."

"What's the history?" I put bags into the cart, since she's standin', talkin'.

"Murder and death, far as you go back. They scalped a bunch of Indians up there two hundred years ago. And history around here means something. People teach their kids around here. We have two local history books in the library. Tell me the name of another small town with two local history books."

"I can't."

"Go to the library and you'll see they have a big display with both books and then that book of lies by Bliesmyer, *Save Her Stupid Bones*. Go look at the pictures in the real history books. You'll see Angus Hardgrave was a McClellan. He has the same exact face."

"I'm convinced."

"And then a hundred years ago the McClellan clan started killing Hardgraves, trying to drive them off. People call it a feud but all it's ever been is McClellan people pushing around Hardgraves until they just scatter and say to hell with it."

"'Cept your brother."

"Well, yeah, but he wasn't a Hardgrave. That's why he had ambition. We had the same father."

She look at me like it dawn on her I'm a nobody, we're in a small town store that don't matter to nobody, and she just won a argument as the sole participant.

"That's a real interesting setup, there. I give you credit for stayin' so collected, like you do. We got a total on the order?"

It's been three minute since she scan the last pork and bean.

She strike a key.

"Two hundred nineteen and forty-one cents."

I peel three bills off a clip. Give 'em to her.

As she drop paper and coin to my hand, a bolt of yellow

cuts the sky outside and the rain quits fallin', and for a second it's just a flash of the last raindrops and steam.

"Thank you, miss…?" I look for a name badge, but alas, only see titties. "Be seein' ya. Good luck on the election. Mebbe you should run instead."

CHAPTER NINE

I GOT GROCERIES HALF UP THE TRUCK CAB, A LITTLE SPACE carved out for the shifter but otherwise its bags on bags to the seat and more. Time I'm two mile outta town it's like they wasn't any rain at all. Road's dry as a bone and leaves float up in the side mirror.

All these middle finger signs for Levi Hardgrave...

Get outta town and it's just road a ways and then my turn.

I pull in slow with the new truck, as Tat don't know I was shoppin' and might shoot me.

"Howdy."

I open the door and since she kinda got a half smile, her eyes reflectin' all that shiny International D1100 paint, I step aside with a swoosh and trail my arm like a magician and make the truck appear.

"What was that?"

"Just a little play, is all. You never see a magician?"

"Oh. Okay."

"That make sense?"

"Enough."

"I bought groceries."

"Let me see. I want pickles."

"You shittin' me? I bought everything in the store twice but pickles."

"Okay."

What?

I'm braced up like to slug it out on account I expect harsh words. Meanwhile, she's mellow and I don't know if I'm the one spoilin' for a fight. Sometimes I don't know my own mind a second, and when I come back it's like I jump forward ten minutes in the conversation, up to where I don't know a single fuckin' thing we was talkin' 'bout. The mind scatter and reassemble in the minutes ahead. I look at Tat and wonder at her, feelin' like I just fended a punch and she's just smilin' at me.

Mood of the forest changed, though, I can tell that. Gettin' dark up the hollow toward the McClellan and Hardgrave lake, like another arm of the storm I just sat through find its way to our corner in the wood.

"You like the truck?"

"Uh. Sure. Where's the food?"

She's lookin' over the bed.

"Passenger side up front."

She circle the grill and looks smilin' and pretty comin' back to the passenger door. I watch her face, see the Indian line and the Spanish, and she's more pert every time she bounce.

Sky flashes as a gust whooshes the upper trees.

Judgin' the storm I sat out in Reynoldsville, if this is a laggin' part of the front, I got to expect it'll make a slick of this place quick. I got the Eldorado sittin' on pure mud, but they's a rock bed up where I got the truck.

Plus, Yank dog's 'bout to get doused.

"Tat, I was in this storm a minute back and it's liable to dump a lake on us. Help me swap the vehicles real quick."

She get behind the wheel in the Cadillac and me the truck. I wave out the window and back out and 'round to the right; she whip the Caddy out the other way, left; I pull forward and she pull forward, and it's good times, like lovers want to step past each other in the hallway, but each move the wrong way and they can't. Spontaneous love with engines and metal.

I stamp the brake and she do too.

See her teeth grinnin' at me from inside the Eldorado.

She wave me ahead and I wave her back more, so I can come forward and back the truck in. She raise both hands. "*Que?*" But I don't lip read Spanish — or I do, enough for one word, but shit if I'm gonna holler through two windshields. Get out the truck and the wind's gustin' solid.

Stinky Joe's ears flap. Carpenter keep his head low.

Hey! You're not forgetting us? Right?

"No, I'm not forgettin'."

I hurry trot to Tat blockin' the road in the Eldorado.

"Need you to back up another vehicle length so I can pull forward and back in."

"Just pull in."

"I want to back in. See?"

"What? It's right there. What?"

"I want to back the truck in so I can get it out easier in case it gets stuck. The truck has four-wheel drive." Look up and the first drop of water lands square on my forehead. "The car don't have four wheel drive. I want the best avenue out is all. I gotta splain this? Back the fuck up."

"What did you say to me?"

"Back the fuck up! I want these vehicles off the road and don't have time —"

She stomp the gas and the car shoot backward. She hit the bank. Eldorado bounce, gold jangle. If she put a dent in the fender bein' a stupid fuckin' girl —

I'll walk away so I don't beat her silly.

That's what I'll do.

I spot her in the windshield still charmin' me with a cold stare and go-fuck-yourself lips.

Step back the truck. Pull forward. Head out the window while I back it up, "Now you just stay where you're at, Joe, and I'll gather both you up. Stay out the way."

I back past the fire circle and keep the wheels on the highs and out the ruts best I can. Tat guns the Caddy engine, blows rocks behind her and comes screechin' up to where the truck was on the road, then cuts the wheel and backs in. I don't see the opposite rear quarter panel 'til she gets the ass swung 'round, and that pristine gold Cadillac Eldorado got a dent like she hit a dump truck.

Don't know if it's the air turned dark and storm-cold, or the electric all about set my mind to sizzlin', but if I don't get some space 'tween me and this woman, I'm liable to regret my actions.

Somethin' in my mind ain't right, and I got a peculiar sense it's to do with this land, the lake, the people.

I open the Eldorado door and come back for Yank dog. On my knees to lift 'im, the old puppydog snarls.

"I was gonna put you in the car!"

Can't you just leave him alone?

"He's gonna get soaked. Can't you smell the rain? C'mon, Yank dog. Let's get you inside."

I scoop under his front legs and he slash up from the side, tooth grab on my cheek and the pain rise quick as I drop him where he lay.

"You son of a bitch."

Baer! What's wrong with you?

Tat's in the Eldorado driver seat twisted and lookin' back through the center and out the door to me and Stinky Joe and Carpenter, layin' back on the dirt.

"Fuck it, is all. Fuck it all."

I step off the same way's the first time I went reconnoiterin', though I know exactly where I'm goin' this time and the only thing 'bout the next hours and days ahead I don't know in a flash is the power that send the realization through me.

"I'm goin' thataway," says I to Tat, lookin' forward so I don't see her face. "That ‑ a ‑ way."

CHAPTER TEN

Up through the hollow with the briar fillin' in where they cut the hardwood and left scrub and hemlock, it ain't a quarter mile to the place I'd camp if I was to homestead this place — and it got a log road cut out all the way to the edge. This place was all hemlock and white pine to begin with, so the hardwood loggers didn't leave it a mess. The rocks is covered in moss so green you could spend it at the dollar store. Hemlock grown old and tall, the lower branches is all busted and fell off long ago.

The woods got a roof but the ceilin's high.

Some the big rocks is like houses and some sit side by side, where it wouldn't take a couple days' labor to frame and fill some livin' quarters 'tween 'em. You can see where the snow'd drift natural, and slope the roof back that way.

Air's humid; sweat run to my chest while I muse on snow. I like the greens back here and the blacks. Crick right there for water.

Rain patter the trees and I wait, mostly dry, while a mountain of water falls through the air 'bout to bury us like in Reynoldsville fifteen-minute back. I ease next the tallest, fattest hemlock and stand with my spine to the bark, head back and eyeballs rotated to the sky, expectin' to find the rain even more interestin' with my head craned half upside-down.

The sky go twilight-dark and wind grunts and howls above; treetops swirl 'round like to make me sick watchin'. I feel power in the trunk behind me — massive — like the electric from the sky and the electric from the ground is meetin' up, and just as I think on how the hair raisin' on the arm and head in the middle of an electric storm has meanin', a bolt of pure white heat flash from the sky and down the tree I'm leanin' on. I see it hover like the Almighty, then *whoosh* down and in. I see it faster'n I can move, but kinda slow motion, and still it's so fast it's nothin' but hot light, the noise of a tree detonatin' like a stick of dynamite and me flailin' and flyin' while the sound of a million volts fryin' the local earthworms fizzles out. I'm still in the air speculatin' the launch was sound with nothin' broke off, but the landin's due to be hell, given the boulder I'm 'bout to drill with my teeth.

But my feet rotate up and 'round and I fly higher still, and shit if I don't bounce 'long the top of that house-size boulder on my backside, then skip like a flat rock off a puddle of cold rainwater, as did the proverbial frog needin' wings to spare his ass.

Whatever cells awoke when my brother Larry try to fry me by shavin' the electric cord, this bolt of lightnin' woke what normal cells remained.

It's as if I see the entire event at once and a second time goin' through it slower, as it happen, so even while that bolt of lightnin' burns my spine and glows every cell to the center of my brain, and my portal to the nonlocal, and the explodin' tree crush agin me so hard my thoughts is left behind, I saw the end as clear as the beginning in the same moment. While I fly toward the house-size rock I'm about to land on, I know I'll get down but the jolt of juice from the sky just recharge my curse such that it won't be only spottin' red eyes and arm juice. Creation was created for truth, such that the unseen world hates untruth; them pockets of denial against the grand scheme sends out ripples and eddies, is why I see the red and feel the juice. This burst of lightnin' gimme 'nother clue to spot the liar in action, and though I don't yet guess the clue, I know I will when I see it.

My whole world's changed.

I take it on faith.

I sense the ground, the air, all of it's tethered to some giant locus the way they say some trees in Africa for miles 'round all got the same roots. Evil's wove like that. And I don't know if it's all Yank country, or just this stretch of woods, the lake, the feudin' families. That blast of electric drop me in a fairy tale.

I lay on the rock with my head rested in a bowl with a pebble at the bottom aggravatin' one spot. I can feel my body's here. They's no pain, and my breathin's 'bout right, and my heart. It's all workin' and I can feel what I ought.

Same time, body's got a vibration all through, and it's like I'm standin' in a pool of water seein' the reflection full of ripples, and closer I look to the feet, closer I get to where I'll see that wavy reflection's 'bout to join the body, and those vibrations'll come right up through, and I won't be able to block 'em out. All the wavelengths of the lies I been spared of seein' by the mercy of the Maker, I'll be spared no more and

I'll see. Every cursed word thought by every man or woman, inside, I'll be privy to not just the spoken lie, but the unspoken to a depth I never see afore.

I see the ripplin' body vibratin' with all that turmoil and see it comin' and I look where the feet meet, and the vibration overtake me like I was dunked in a pool.

All that's mind of me, all that's pure thought, is zapped through black space.

I come to feelin' like I been gone a thousand year, on my back with rain spatterin' my face.

I pat Smith.

Good.

Black clouds straight above, but no voices in the mind, no thoughts ongoin', just open my eyes and see. I give the moment a chance to unfold. Next couple, too. Feel the heartbeat, steady. The breathin', steady. Got that fuckin' flashin' pain at the pebble holdin' up the back of my head. Cancel that out and feel the bones press rock, get a sense of how gravity's a blessin', as I don't want to float off.

After a good ten second, I get my bearin's and rather'n try and sit up, I lift my right foot as if in this new world the ground has an obligation to meet it.

It don't, this world. Which make me suspect I come back to the same world I left.

I elevate my right arm and bend the elbow. My left is equally flexible. Buckle the right knee and pull the thigh. All good. The left. And that fuckin' pebble at the back of my head gets through, and I think hell with it and all at once, stand.

On top a rock, no good way to get down, maybe twenty feet.

Wind's passed. Rain's thinned to a steady drip. I stretch

this way and that, surprised no parts is missin', broke or burnt. Growin' up, I heard of a man blasted right off the John Deere in the field; had light-holes out his feet and couldn't carry a pocket watch. That was him. For me, a couple bones in my back been givin' me a shit seems knocked back in line with one 'nother, so on the whole it I come out dandy.

Air got a chill. My clothes is soppy and I'd like to levitate off this rock afore the next blast of rain. The clouds is angry black, flashed with fury. I step to the closest edge. Thirty feet, slopin' to maybe twenty at the low end. I follow the edge, lookin' a channel down, a crevice, a tree.

Nothin'.

Come to the bottom corner and if I had young legs I'd jump. I judge it'd take less'n three second to hit, and any young man can't survive three seconds floatin' in the air is just a pussy, is all.

Since I ain't a young man and I got a bum leg and a hipbone feels dipped in dirt, all I'll give myself is a one-second fall. Estimated. Like the time it take to jump one rock crossin' the crick to another. Longer fall 'n that, I'll take a couple week and braid a rope outta moss.

Keep followin' 'round.

On the last wall headed back up the high side of the boulder, they's a smaller boulder shoulderin' up, with a dead tree leanin' next it, so if I can make the ten-foot drop without bustin' an ankle, I can most likely navigate the next fifteen or so easier.

I give the question to the clouds and rain: is this fall gonna take more'n a second? And the clouds and rain say *get the fuck off the rock*.

I jump.

Fall take precisely one second. I lead with my good leg, roll right, upslope and back toward the main boulder so I don't spin over the edge. The joints flash a bit of wary pain; make sure the systems is workin', but nothin' breaks and I regain my feet all but convinced that electric thunderbolt left me pert near invincible.

Down on my knees at the edge over the leanin' tree, I pull a piece of dry rotted wood off the stump. It's been dead as long as Lincoln and what branches the tree had is mostly fell off. It's more 'n a second to the ground, but the ground is springy woods dirt, not rock, and if I can slide partways down this rotted tree afore it give out, or I tumble off, that's the recommended fall right there.

Have to be a weak ass tree, weight bearin' almost vertical, not to support a man. Especially one in need and favored by the nonlocal.

Pat Smith one more time. Always thought Yosemite Sam had an idea worth tryin', that levitatin' six-shooters move, but it'd likely take more Turkey to make it workey.

Shouldn't be nervous 'bout this.

I look up. Black clouds move fast like a army 'cross the sky got someplace to be. But long as I look they's no relentin'. Wherever this storm come from, it's got a lot pushin' behind it. So I get on fours, park the ass out where the wind can have at it and drop a leg over the edge. Grab one hand on the dry-rotted tree as my foot finds a nub, and I get it planted solid 'nough I can get my other hand on the tree too.

The nub snaps off and I drop.

First hand on the tree's grippin' mulch and now I'm fallin' with my nuts ridin' center as the tree bend out from the rock. I rake 'em over a knot like to rip the jewels out the bag, and just as the vomit pain overtake me, somethin' smart from the void rush into my mind, a fuzzball of meanin', and I clamp both elbows and arms on the rotted tree like elevator brakes and my fall slows to when the last knot hits my thigh, it bounce me and the jewels free to drop the last three feet with no further testicular torment.

I land in a rain puddle lined with last year's leaves, cup my hands over my genetic package and I'm ready to trade up. This one feel busted to shit.

Exhale long and slow. Close the eyes as the raindrops hit 'em. Tiny fists all over the face, ice cold, punch with a sting.

Kinda nice, while the rest of the body want to curl up and gag.

Can't tell if that's water on my thigh and groin, or if I ripped out the femoral, and these stunned seconds in the rain is my last. Slip the hand inside my drawers, down the leg and 'round expectin' warm and sticky blood, but all I feel is hard-water rain and a mighty miracle of torment from whichever of my nuts feels busted to smithereens.

I clear the throat of a little sample of yack, taste coffee, swallow it back down where it'll do some good.

I'm alive. Heartbeat. Lungs movin' in and out. Got the brain, all seems in order there. Only thing wrong is I'm likely de-testiculated, and the supreme fuckery of it is I can't jump headlong off the boulder as I already come down the fuckin' thing.

But let's see if I can stand.

I flop to the side but my balls is somethin' else entirely.

This is gonna take a minute. Worst comes to worst, I left my knife so I'll have to shoot 'em off, get some relief.

I close my eyes and let the thinkin' roam.

I like the land.

The thought comes the way of insight gleaned from punishment, meanin' it's hateful learnin'. Like the time Mrs. Sprague made me stay after school at the chalkboard writin' *I will not shoot spitballs in class* a hundred thousand times if a hundred. Time I was done, I start thinkin' how bein' virtuous and wholesome might be worth checkin' out.

Hateful learnin', achieved under duress.

Still, I do like the land.

Thought arrives like the land itself said so, and I think on how that could be, and likely is the way it works in general. The land tellin' us things we never slow down 'nough to hear.

Slow down.

If I don't move but keep my sphincter puckered and my stomach tight, the mawin' pain of my busted nut's survivable, and I can let the thoughts drift a minute. Give the jewels time to do what they gotta do.

Yeah, slow down.

I like the land and the people got a mystery to 'em.

I find the locus of the evil, maybe…

Maybe I stomp it out.

Once I crawl out the crucible.

CHAPTER ELEVEN

Spot a porcupine ten feet up a birch, gnashin' his jaw and lookin' through gray hairs to the rain, got perseverance in the eye. Porcupine's a fuck-it-drive-on kinda animal. Gotta respect the quilly son of a bitch.

Wish I had teeth like that. Flexibility.

Lay on my side so long the shoulder hurt, and I got to flop to the other to get my neck straight. Next, to my back and I lay and watch the gray and black clouds swirlin'. Keep the lids squinted agin the rain but it's no use. They's enough drops, one two slaps the eyeballs every couple second. Enough to drive a man to drink — and not the water comin' out the sky. All the agony and the tears in my vision give me the same displacement as a half decent drunk, and a thought occurs so profound I say it aloud.

"While I suffer I ain't as much myself as I truly am."

And it seem like the point of the whole world, the pinpoint

of truth to make sense of it all, lay in some random brain pressed agin the mud, covets death in secret.

"While I suffer I ain't as much myself as I truly am."

Drive my head agin the mud and grit the teeth. Hold back another volley of coffee, bread and bacon grease. That pain in my sack is otherworldly and I can only let my thoughts go on a bit...

The world don't give a shit for preservin' information, make it easier for the next generation. I walk out in front a truck on the highway, it'll maybe take a year or ten thousand for the next Baer to get electro zapped into enlightenment, and if he don't have the presence of mind to bring a tablet or something, who know how long it'll take for the wisdom to percolate through society.

They's likely things some people know that I don't, that would matter if I did. Wish the fuck I knew how to know.

I bet Stinky Joe knows things I don't.

Ruth, I bet.

Tat.

I close my eyes and give 'em a rest from the peltin' rain and after a minute or five the mind's so far adrift, I get this glowy feelin', backa my forehead. This spooky thought-gravity, somethin'. Like my thinkin' has a place associated but mapped with entirely different coordinates than a man'll use for ordinary two plus two brain work.

The gravity's like a different place as much as a different force, and the knowledge expands so I understand it's on account the thinkin' ain't mine. This is another kind of learnin', not the hateful spiteful shit a man'll pick up when another teach him to bend the knee and kiss the ring. This is elevated thinkin', divine wizardly thinkin', from a deeper world'n the one I know. And *with the eyes shut* I see that same gray-browed porcupine, and he got a little snarl to the nose and what was hid from me with my eyes open is apparent with 'em shut. His body got a flicker, like an old television. He come and go, there then he ain't, and after four five flickers he climb 'round the tree.

A signal afore the act.

While I ponder the vision, I get to wonderin' if the real porcupine had the gray eyebrows, or the one I imagine. I got to see the real animal agin.

I open the eyeballs. Rest my stare on that porcupine. Just as I register the gray eyebrows, he fuckin' flickers...

He fuckin' flicker like a television.

I smack my face three times. Cup water from a rock puddle and splash my face even wetter.

That porcupine disappear and come back. And while he's gone, I see the tree behind.

Usetacould trust the eyeballs and now they's gone too. Hairy—as in danger hairy. Can't trust the written word nor the spoken and now the porcupine disappear. I wonder if cow shit still stinks, or if that rule's out the window too.

But even as I think it, I get the insight the eyeballs is dead on the money, it's my world I can't trust, and when the porcupine ain't there, he very well fuckin' ain't there.

It's the perception been improved. I see faster, somethin'. More juice maybe?

Whatever it is I'm seein', it's true. That animal disappear. We all disappear, I suspect I'll learn.

I can't ken it all the way, but I suspect I'm seein' through mystic eyes. Some them preachers in Virginny like to charm the snakes and get close the Lord thataway. You got the women in Greece, up in the mountains eatin' grapes and throwin' orgies back in the day. They got Buddha people over there, you know. Go into the trance a hundred year and come out with them long white whiskers. They's ten thousand ways folk've figured out to plug into the Higher Authority, whichever name they give it. I was a kid they like to use the drugs. Tune in. And now I got the juice from the nonlocal, gimme the perception of the animal's changin' intentions. He look at me content as a sonofabitch, eyeball to eyeball, and zap flash zoop, he go 'round the tree.

I know what to make of it.

Been layin' in cool rainwater long 'nough a chill start in the spine and start jerkin like to make waves in a rope. Come on me so fast I got no control but manage to buzz and jiggle myself standin' while the body shiver and shake to get warm.

While the Greek god Testaclees writhe and roll, down below.

Grab a birch and once I'm steady, keep walkin' the direction I was headed when I said, *That a way*. I go birch to birch and switch to cherry and maple here 'n there, through a tiny acre of hardwood hid from the logger, tucked back agin the interstate highway. The motion gimme control; long as I'm movin' the shivers is null. Each swing of the left leg I get a jolt of death up the spine and it won't be many hours of this afore I'll put a stop to it whichever way leaves the smallest mess.

That's a literal thought, and the realization gimme ambition. Can't think of many things I'd avoid more'n castration, and while I give it a frank think, I lean on a boulder at the base of the slope leadin' up to the highway.

What about castration to save your life?

Fuck that.

So they ain't but two acceptable solutions: life or death. Regardless, the nuts stay attached.

Could I give up one if it was crushed like a cherry tomato?

I dunno 'bout that. Man get by with one lung and you don't call him a pussy.

Longer I lean, standin', the more my stomach turn.

Leadin' off at the bank to the interstate above, I launch and give the sack a jostle, and the bread and bacon grease I ate come up with the coffee that chase it. The thrustin' and shakin' launch new waves of torture and I scramble up and forward like a madman searchin' an eighteen-wheeler to end his misery. But it's a mighty feat climbin' the bank and at the top I'm whooped enough to sit on the guardrail, rather'n find a Mack on the other side. It'd be a good time to seek the woods on the other side the highway, as they's no traffic for a mile comin'. But I don't want to step onto the concrete 'til I know if my purpose is to cross it or to paint it.

The metal like to cut a new crack in my ass so I shift back and lay on the grass with my head low 'nough it'd take a hawk in the driver seat for anyone passin' by to spot me. Don't need to vomit as much as afore, a victory I'll accept with greed. I close the eyes and ponder the last minutes and hours.

What the fuck's goin' on in Yank country?

Land's possessed.

Am I willin' to die in Yank country?

CHAPTER TWELVE

No. No I ain't.

I pull the right knee forward and push off so I'm half standin'. No cars comin' in a long way, though I see 'em. I get the right leg over the guard rail and sit a second, but that flares the pain in my nutsack so I launch from there. Halfway 'cross the interstate I sense doom, though the car is still a good ways off. But I look agin and the car is damn near on me, and I got to hoof it.

To preserve the magic of momentum I rush over the rail and down the gulley, now lookin' back the other way for the traffic comin' on the eastbound lane.

It's clear.

I'm winded as shit.

But it's clear and if I don't get up now, I'll be throwin' up anyway. So, I shove off up the slope, stumble, collect myself, get over the guardrail and look.

Now they's two tractor trailers barrelin' in. One got the flat nose is in the close lane. Other with a cab like a dog's head is in the far.

Pretty sure I can make it across.

I push off and regret that shit right away. But it'd be harder to turn 'round 'n keep shovin' forward, one stomp at a time, with every time my sack hits a thigh bein' pure hell.

Them trucks is comin'.

One horn.

Two horn.

I'm pushin' all I got and look to the side and see a bunch of flashes inside the truck cab, like a strobe, and the rig start bouncin' as the man hop on the brakes and the wheels go stiff.

I bound off the concrete and over the rail. Truck's bouncin' still, got the window down and I hear cussin' like from somewhere they speak city. No poetry to it.

Even with the truck well past, that driver's pissed and I think he's liable to hop out the rig and see if he can shoot me. I race sideways down the bank, easier to go at full speed and not get ahead the self, and easier on my punji wound in my calf, 'cept the legs movin' side to side ain't at all like the legs movin' front to back, so far as a pair of sore danglin' nuts is concerned.

Muhammad Ali workin' a speed bag.

My situation, down there.

Keep racin' down the bank and into the woods, get past the low hemlock up front and then do some ziggin' and zaggin' 'tween them fat tree trunks. Dare you to shoot me.

Shit.

I *wish* you'd shoot me.

But I keep on.

Longer I hold the pace, more my stomach get dull to it. I

feel each bounce and jostle, but like a twisted ankle once it ain't so mobile.

I walk a bit and come on a crick. Pain's local now; each step don't make the stomach sick too. At the crick I figure that truck driver like as not already drove off. He was flashin' lightin' inside, like that disappearin' porcupine, show me what it look like to change the mind.

Now, if I'm alone, and got ice cold-crick water flash floodin' the crickbed...

If I got in a pocket over where the flow curls slow 'round the pool...

I'd be safe all around and maybe get some relief...

If I was to drop my drawers and let my entire scrotal mess, *per se*, soak in that summer ice water from the sky.

Rigorous analysis complete, I drop my drawers and squat to a rock a couple inch in under the water and sit.

The jewels rejoice.

I can tell on account the ragin' pain's all gone and the dull ache is settlin' back farther from mind.

Who the hell was it told me that story 'bout dick fishin'? Where I hear that?

Regardless, that torrent of rain's a damnsight less intense in a forest than a town. Time it percolates through the hemlock or whatever else... They got a lot a cherry and beech. Time the rain get to ground level, the drops come thick and slow, and feel more like kisses from heavy girls 'n them narrow zingers come rippin' out the open sky, feel like a shot from a pellet gun.

Ooooh — eeee my balls.

This cold water's real nice.

A squirrel wasn't payin' me no mind alla sudden jump to a maple and disappear behind.

Drop my hand to Smith. Get a notion they's no need, so I put my fingers back in the water.

Leaves and feet on the bank above, then a man step close 'nough to spot me over the ledge.

He don't point his pistol. His lungs is workin' hard.

"You!"

"Me?" says I.

"Ya fuckin' near got a lotta people killed."

He's a big fella — is why it took so long to find me.

"I got a lotta fuckin' weight on that rig. You know what it takes to stop that much weight?"

"How much weight?"

"Forty fuckin' tons, is how much. You know how much weight that is? *Fuck!*"

He turn sideways and fume thataway, and I discover from the depths of my new insights it's a courtesy, him turnin' away while he's all fustered up and ready to cluck. He don't want that poison' gettin' on me while he ain't got his mind made up.

Thinkin' he was ready for war and seein' me in the cool pool got him confused enough to point his meanness aside, like a fella who ain't sure he wants to shoot somebody'll often point the gun elsewhere. Same exact phenomenon, and it's enlightenin' to see proof of what I always suspect: if cussin' a plant'll kill it, then cussin' a man'll put a burden on him too, and he better know more 'n a plant how to deal with it.

I do all that perceivin' in a blip.

Meanwhile he's wearin' cut off overalls, and his legs don't look healthy is the only way to say it. But he's a brawny somebody and my pants is soaked and bunched. Got Smith hangin' ready out the holster danglin' off my knees.

He see it.

That zappin' state he was in back there, bouncin' in the cab, is over. I got to assume he's still on the warpath he chose in the moment. He don't understand the situation.

"Friend, you don't understand the situation."

He raise his gun on me. I don't like it.

"I'm not your friend," says he.

"Humor me. And I don't care if you don't got any humor. Borrow some of mine. Which means quit runnin' your dick licker a minute."

He stare.

"Good. Okay. You see I got my stones in the crick water. That's on account the water's cold. I want my nuts cold on account I was next a tree got hit by lightnin'. That zap both the tree and me, and launch me, and time I come down I'm ridin' a log and just about de-testiculate myself. You understand. I made that word up but it seems pretty fuckin' obvious someone else shoulda made it up by now."

He still starin'.

I lift my hand off my jewels and maybe the water add a little magnification. From where I look, I got a grapefruit down there.

Part my knees. His vantage, I bet it's a honeydew.

Says I, "Tell me I ain't justified in any mad pursuit come to mind, to get a handle on the torment."

I watch while he ponder, and most times in the past if I care what someone's thinkin', I'll watch the face for signals and trust the red eyes and juice to warn of any treachery afoot.

Now I don't know how to perceive him. Play it by ear, I guess.

He nods, slow.

"All right. You understand. Put the gun down at least, if you ain't sure you seen enough to go 'bout your business."

He was noddin' his head but stop, and now his eyes is a little narrower, and his lips a little thinner, and his nose perk up, and he look like Roy Clark pretendin' to be Elvis.

I spot a tinge of red in his eyes.

And then the snarly look disappear and he do the porcupine skizzle - flash, that staticky disappearin' act, and watchin' this dodgy Brooklyn fella it ain't so much as I'm seein' a different him. It's like earlier with the porcupine. I'm seein' better, and more, with faster eyes.

I spot the trees behind him six eight times in a half second, and I know that's the moment he change intent. He got his instructions from wherever he get 'em, and all that's left is for him to execute.

Did he change his mind? Or someone change it for him?

Dunno.

I dunno what I just saw, 'cept it was mindfulness, or *intent* aimed like a gun, and after that, a dismissal like I ain't a stranger no more, half naked with my nuts in the water.

I see a man thinkin' he's thinkin' and ain't, is what I saw.

That hangs over my ill-humor like another shadow a minute, while I wonder on how many folks is like that all the time, got the program, got the lies, don't even know. Just pointin' that intent all over the place, finger on the trigger.

It ain't the nonlocal that's spooky. It's this fuckin' place.

The sound of Brooklyn's feet on soggy leaves and twigs disappear after two steps.

Sizable chunk of wood float by the main crickway. My pool's startin' to foam like laundry detergent. I stand a quick minute and investigate. The boys is like a peach picked a month early. I'll soak'm a few more minute and if the foam reach me, I suppose I'll have to scrub my armpits.

Gimme somethin' to do while I ponder the human condition and my nuts.

UP OUT THE WATER, I SHED MY DRAWERS. RAIN'S STOPPED but the sky's still black 'nough it don't feel like a full reprieve. Regardless, I get out my boots then roll and squeeze my britches, empty out as much crick water as possible and they feel six pound lighter when I put 'em back on. Next, I strip the insoles out my boots, set boots upside down agin a rock to drain, while I arm-whip the water out the insoles. Then my socks. Reassemble and step off from the crick feelin' almost brand new. Armpits is clean and Tide fresh. My stone sack ain't so aggravated and I don't know if maybe both my nuts got a good thumpin, rather than one gettin' busted.

Maybe the nonlocal can send my nads some love.

I turn a circle. Orient myself.

Thinkin' back on that feller from the highway, if that's all the new curse is, I don't see what's to fear. It's just a little zappin'. Keep things interestin', and if I'm in a situation, things is lookin' good, and I see that flashy shit goin' on, then I'll know aheada time, maybe the red eyes and juice is comin'. Like that flashy shit's a pre-warnin' system.

I'll take it.

But that ain't the superpower I'da chose new off the shelf.

Bearin's got, I head out. Raindrops keep droppin' now, though the rain out the sky's long quit. It's all the rain stored in the leaves filterin' down.

I step out the woods to the back of a decrepit orchard. If these apple trees was farm animals, any decent man 'd put 'em down. With a hammer if he had nothin' else.

What a miserable mess of fruit trees.

It's like walkin' through one of Jesus's parables, all these bad fruit trees, and I think on the gnashin' of teeth I been doin', on account of my busted sack, and I get to wonderin' if Someone ain't doin' a remake of Job, like sometimes in Hollywood they'll take a film that was pretty fuckin' bad the first go 'round, then see if they can make it worse.

This is the dead candidate's land.

Up on the right — though I can't see over the dome, comin' up through the orchard the hill ain't round yet — but over thataway's gonna be the burned barn I saw on the other hill, walkin' earlier. And that put the house square ahead, maybe a little to the right. No, a little more still to the right.

I come over the top and it's more orchard up a short ways, then lawn, then the house.

Off the right is the charred joists and timbers of the barn. I cross the land feelin' like I'm walkin' through square inches fraught with history and import, every one. Such as a woman was murdered on this inch where I stand, and over where you're at, it was a young boy met his untimely end.

In my mind it's like walkin' on a acre of ancient skulls, gettin' to the house.

I'm walkin' through grass ain't been mowed in months and another level of perception layers in, the way I can almost hear the tinkle of crushed skull bone under foot, each step, as the sins stored in the land bust open and the ghosts of all those murdered souls rush out, seekin' justice. I don't know what I see versus what I imagine. The clouds lighten a bit, and the black is moved on; though the mists just a hundred feet off the ground tumble and swirl into the bigger clouds flowin' just above, so the whole air shimmers with gray light.

All the ghosts disappear as I put my foot to the step and climb, like me enterin' this house sends a signal I ain't the one them souls was lookin' for.

One, two, three. Stand on the porch, look off to the right, to the ruined barn. Look off the porch to my left, and it's that giant lake I saw from above, now I'm seein' it from the very end, so it looks to go on and on almost forever, with the eventual bend comin' so far off, it's a shadow in mist.

It strikes me that evil loves a pretty scene, maybe more 'n the good.

At the door I reach and realize I ain't felt my nuts in a bit, and I don't know if that's good. So afore grabbin' the handle I grab my sack, give the container a good go round, and with certifiable utmost care, thump each nut.

Rightey—he ain't feelin' too good yet. On the mend, need a nap. Leave him be.

Leftey—he doin' much better. He caught the second busted branch and Rightey already had the factory shoved half up my ass by then, so he was protected.

Don't know exactly what I was suppose to learn in today's lesson, or if it concluded.

I open the door to the Hardgrave house.

CHAPTER THIRTEEN

I step inside the livin' room and don't know exactly why I stand where I stand. Which ain't nothin' as I also confess I don't understand why I do any of what I do these days, or these minutes, since Tat tell me she's growin' my son in her belly.

My boy's name is Moxie.

But that don't feel like the world I'm lookin' inside, right now.

Musty air in the house. That girl — the dead man's sister — girl with the nice rack at the grocery store checkout — say it only been a few days, yet they's no crime scene at the house far as I can see. Don't look like they was any commotion. No boots draggin' in grass and dirt. No blood brushed agin the wall on accident.

My last year I smell fifty-six dead.

This house don't smell like death.

Make a fella wonder where this Hardgrave candidate was

standin' when he put the gun to his head. Or where he was when someone else put it there. My first thought when his sister said he didn't off himself was he did it inside the house, but if that's the case the house's been cleaned. And if it was cleaned, how'd they get it to look old and dingy and un-givashit-about?

That look can't be rushed, and just a little Clorox'll make it disappear.

First thing noticeable in the living room is the fireplace. It's big and ugly: two posts stickin' out the field stones for mountin' old muskets. Kitchen to the right. I find a glass behind the third cupboard door and fill it at the sink. Lean on the counter and drink that water down. Though my belly's full, the mouth's dry and not sticky, like to smack the tongue, but pasty, like to stick the tongue to the roof of the mouth and leave it there all day.

Thirsty, is all.

Truth told, deep, deep, down I got a notion like afore when I knew Brooklyn wouldn't be trouble with his gun. I don't know its source, only that the notion's guidin' my steps with an end in mind, and we'll arrive together if I let things run.

Check the cabinet under the sink.

Ammonia. Scrub pads. Dish soap, the spare bottle with the lavender scent. Next door over is the pots and pans for bakin'.

Next is a row of drawers, then the dishwasher. I climb off the knees and now doin' a full turn, slower, I spot what I shoulda been lookin' all along: the hutch.

It's at least a thousand-year-old, made of wormy chestnut I bet, and one of the hinges is fixed with a piece of brass coat hanger, bent at each end.

Bottom door open, I pull two jugs of black liquid and soon

as my fingers touch the glass I can tell the potion inside is divine, but wicked, and the moment I drink it I won't know good and evil the way I do now.

I'll know it with more insight 'n any man ever lived save the one walked on water. I'll see into souls and like epoxy needs the two sides to bind, I'll know the full light and dark in every man, woman, child or dog I look at, the way maybe Eve did when she drug mankind into sin and sufferin', on account her nebbin' in the Garden.

A harsh read on Genesis, I confess.

But I'll see the whole of the human peeled back, and what's dark and light in each.

Seems more truth 'n any man's built to handle. The prospect is hateful. I don't want any part.

I leave the jugs on the table where I sit 'em.

Back away like I stumble on a nest of rattlers, slow, so neither them jugs leap in my hand, uncap itself and fill my throat with poison.

But a good six feet off I'm feelin' safe and drop my guard. Give the concept a fair think. Seems like learnin' from beyond, bigger'n anything I'd fancy on my own. I can almost see an old man's face. That learnin' says *go get a swaller of that likker, if you want to see the soul of industry and power. It's in your path to do so.*

"I don't give a fuck for the soul of industry. Nor power," says I aloud, though I suspect the voice can hear my thinkin' as easy as my spoken words.

This place crawls with the spooky.

But my prints is on those jugs, and let's say that middle finger campaign girl runs for office in her brother's place, and wins, and she want a new investigation. Then they find my fingerprints and that's one more murder they add to the list.

That's a good point right there. A good argument.

In the pragmatic sense, I could give a shit. The pragmatic sense is familiar with that stance.

But in the deprive-bad-luck-of-oxygen line of thinkin', leavin' my fingerprints on them jugs is pure showin' my ass, donuts in the parkin' lot kinda behavior. Risky, pure and simple. 'Specially since I didn't murder the man my prints would evidence I did.

I better get them jugs off the table, is all.

Mindful not to fall prey to seductive visions, I do my best to not think on how much I enjoy a good drunk. I don't want to be next them jugs thinkin' and wishin' I was intoxicated.

I make sure not to muse on the way likker take the edge off people's voices, improves most boobs, no matter how good they was sober, and makes water wetter and sunshine warmer.

Look at a frog drunk, and it'll be more froggy. Regardless which of you's drunk.

Now I got these jugs in my hands I don't know what to do with 'em. I can't dump the contents down the sink. Not while they's sober kids in Africa.

I rest 'em on the end table by the sofa. Sit on the edge and watch my hand uncap the first. I don't rest that jug on my shoulder for a proper slug o' shine but grip the neck like a chicken I want to throttle, and get the openin' close enough for a good whiff.

I been thinkin' all wrong, just assumin' on account the visions and whatnot that whatever liquid was in this jug had some force to it, maybe associated with the locus of evil and mischief I been sensin'. I been suspicious of this likker on account this whole terrain is kooky.

But I ain't some third stringer brought in on account the

first two got a case of the pussies. I'm the ringer. A distiller by trade, recruited into the service of the forces of good in their perpetual and everlastin' battle agin evil.

I don't wait for war; I bring it.

I'm on a mission, and that means sometimes I got to buck up and do what I got to do.

I lift that green glass gallon of black whiskey to my mouth and tip back my head. Elevate the ass of that jug 'til a tiny, tiny splash of heat land in my mouth and I ease back and fully savor the sample. Mouth's kinda numb, like I drunk a vapor. But the clammy sticky feelin' disappear and every tastebud on my tongue tingles.

'Cept the ones that's numb.

I touch my tongue to the glass agin. Anticipation. Tip the jug farther. Lean back more. The balance shift and a giant slug o' shine hit the back my throat and the fire put me half in surprise and half in delight. But I keep the jug aloft a second too long, and spill liquid joy in the windpipe.

This's as close to two hundred proof as I've drunk, and I can tell from the narcosis on my tongue, it ain't alcohol doin' all the work.

They's somethin' else doin' some liftin' in there, some ingredient taste rotted out, like moldy walnuts, somethin'. It's from the dark side I can tell right off. It's got a disorganized feel, not like a comfortable bedroom with clothes and nonsense all over the place but disorganized like a bomb. Like chaos or buildings fallin' down. Things that matter no longer matterin'. Things that produce, no longer producin'. Things that love turnin' to hate. That likker's dark in a way I never see, its motive so clear.

Use to wonder as a boy, after I started spottin' the lies

comin' at me from all directions, why folks'd say so many. I see now it wasn't fit for a boy to perceive such a perverted and ugly truth, and I'm glad I never understood.

Some folk love to build and they build things and people both. They's a product at the end the labor. Food to eat. A place to stay. Warm thighs and love. Wisdom for tomorrow. We add. We're alive. That's good. Let's make more life and smell a flower every day, even if everything else is shit. We move forward that way, though sometime it maybe feels we're slippin' backward.

But other folk find livin' hateful. They don't love to build but they do love to eat, and that set 'em at odds. Competing wills tear down the house. That's what the Almighty said. Servin' two masters: one for the appearance, so he can keep eatin', and the other playin' out the long-term suicide, settin' booby traps, dippin' darts in poison, tellin' lies and sowin' disorder out of resentment over the simple fact he ain't and can't be true.

If a fella hates himself that's likely as honest as he gets.

That very force of darkness swirls in the air afore me, like a tendril of black smoke from a candle, only it accumulates while it flows 'bout the room. I don't know what to make of my mortal self at the moment.

I see the same with my eyes closed as open, a room with a giant-ass coil of black smoke all around me.

I lean on the table.

That smoke got a personality. That smoke is a somebody.

Rest the jug I drank outta on my leg, finger still through the loop.

This ain't the great satan, as they sometimes call him, in the smoke.

It's a lesser demon.

My divine intuition says I found the locus I felt from the hills and my stumblin' ain't a matter of chance. I'm here and equipped with only what's needed for the appointment, and if I don't have any tools but Smith and my rural sophistication, that's on account they's unnecessary and extra weight.

But these jugs full of cursed liquid...

I'll teach you the ways of country commerce.

"Fuck you."

I'm the weakest man alive to trust with not gettin' lost in the intoxication.

But I'm the ringer.

I got this.

I back out the kitchen with a jug hung off each index finger, and my eyes on the evil manifest in the swirlin' smoke.

I can get you laid.

"I need no assistance."

I see his old, bitter face in the smoke. That fucker's name come to me out the ether but I won't say it.

I back out the living room door and stand on the porch lookin' in, my clothes still drippin', my nuts still cryin' for healin'.

Careful with the walnut whiskey.

As I wonder at all that's gone on, me talkin' at the smoke, the snake of black fades to gray, and in another second dissolves into what shadows and darkness was already in my field of view: the black at the corners of the steps, the shadows in the fireplace, any crevice where darkness lurk in the open. All that evil pours into the room's lines and shadows and disappears, and that's how it's always around us.

I step back, and back more, troublin' to watch where I'm

leavin' more 'n where I'm goin', on account I don't fully yet comprehend what evil I face.

And now that I'm on the dirt lookin' up, the Hardgrave house looks the same as I first saw it, and if I didn't have two jugs tuggin' my elbows, I'd suspect I took a nap at the interstate rest stop and been dreamin' since then.

Don't take your time coming back to see me.

"Like I said. Go fuck yourself."

CHAPTER FOURTEEN

I come back the same way I left. Tat's got a tarp stretched from the Eldorado, weighted with rocks on the trunk. She did all that afore the rain start.

Joe's under the trunk and Yank dog's in the space behind Tat, and though his blanket's wet at the edge it look like Tat kept all three of 'em dry.

She watch me arrive from the wood carryin' jugs. Crushin' mushy twigs. I nod at the Yank dog — Carpenter. Tat's rubbin' his foot and my eyes fool me a second: I see black on her face, like what snaked 'bout the walls back at the Hardgrave house.

"He gettin' better, or worse? And he can hear what you say, you know. Stinky Joe too."

Yank Dog don't look up, but Stinky Joe's pawed forward and he do. Tat shake her head sideways.

Yank Dog ain't doin' too hot.

Stinky Joe look solemn, and some folk say a dog'll know long before a man when a soul leaves the earth. Just as I suspect Yank dog's 'bout to shed his mortal ass and slip into the ether, I get a nudge back the mind says maybe it ain't the Yank dog needs to say his goodbyes.

Could be anyone, rate people die 'round me.

I rest the jugs on the International bed then drop the tailgate and sit to give 'em company.

Tat say, "What is that, in the jugs? Oil?"

"Whiskey."

"Wonderful."

I swallow somethin' foul off the tip of my tongue to keep me from sayin' it. But I suspect I'll burp a feather or two. Bein' a woman, Tat won't be able to let what I said lay.

I wait…

"Just what we need," Tat say. "Whiskey."

My best cuttin' words is bunched in my mouth for spittin', but just as I face Tat, I stop. She's like normal, busty these days, got that knocked up glow so her prettiness is all but unbearable seen head on. Sideways more so. Only thing to do is poke her, lookin' like that. But through that glowy light swims a shadow, and while it cross her face the darkness splinters into a swarm of baby snakes twistin' about like that old man in the Hardgrave house just minutes ago. Resentment and anger tunnel her face like black veins, and I hear the thoughts that fill her heart with poison:

He doesn't care that he's about to become a father. I'm insane! What have I done? He's older than my father! He's an alcoholic. He's lazy and smells. His dick hurts me. He has a death wish and he's insane. Really insane. Not like flipping out insane. The dog doesn't even like him. He is a selfish man. He got Corazon killed. He isn't safe to be near.

Her thinkin' never stops. She got that nonsense tumblin' in her mind over and over and it don't matter if it *wasn't* true, she's sayin' enough it'd *be* true. I don't even parse the words, after a couple give me the flavor. I let 'em spill through my awareness, nonstop, 'til I cut her off.

"Stop!"

She got the creative madness to her face; don't even know she's castin' black spells every place she look. Hexin' people. And that woman got my son in her belly.

"What?"

"Stop thinkin' a minute, so I can. You're goin' nonstop."

"I haven't said a word. Oh my God."

"What you say? What now?"

"You hear what people think. Corazon said you could."

Think a minute.

"That ain't exactly true."

I can't hardly tolerate lookin' at her, but I do. The black crawlers on her face, it's like sometimes you can see the mold behind the next layer of onion. You got to take another off to be safe, and for your trouble you got an onion.

Most natural thing in the world, I uncap the jug I already sampled, fit it to the elbow, upend and open the flowgates straight to the belly. Try not to gulp, as that'll only slow the torrent. Need somethin' wild, help me make sense or numb me to what don't.

I get a bellyful of that hateful shine and it's like I'm in the Old Testament and got to do somethin' stupid, gin up some punishment. It's like that, and it ain't. Some of that mean shit tickles me to do it. Stupid action earns stupid consequences and I delight seein' 'em unfold.

The deeper truth is I like killin' wicked people. Spent my whole life convinced I was evil for wishin' wickedness on 'em.

But these last few months I come to see the true harmony of it.

In general society, it ain't good for folk to think like I do.

Can't have three hundred million destroyers. We ain't built to be the mainstay, the people what make society produce the goods and generate all them numbers to keep track of. Sweat and toil and pay the bills.

Destroyers is set apart.

Ordinary folk ain't constructed for it. You gotta be busted to be a killer, even ordained. I was made for it, is the point, as no man troubles himself to do anything without incentive.

Tat catch my eye and we lock a long second or three.

I think it's the wicked likker lettin' me see the full scope: though I kept the smiley Baer in Tat's face these last months, she's seen the other. She knew my mind this whole time — clear — as I only now come to know hers: *he got Corazon killed. He isn't safe to be around.*

That shine hits like an iron skillet to the temple and leaves my thoughts back where my brain was clocked. I hope to get back to 'em, as I wanted to remind myself of somethin'.

"Hey there, you uh, Sweet Beanpole. It'll be all right. I kinda like this land, you know?"

"What are you talking about?"

"The dog. Nature'll take its course. You bein' a woman, and you know, got the baby comin', you got all kinda mixed up feelin's. And it's only natural a sick dog'd get you feelin' blue."

"What the fuck, Baer?"

"Huh?"

"You just blow up and leave? Storm coming? Sick dog? And you're so drunk you can't even remember what you did two seconds ago? What the fuck?"

"Now hold your panties on."

"Oh, funny. Wonderful."

"But not in a bunch."

"You leave the first time and you come back with a truck. Bossy big man gets so mad he runs into the woods. And comes back drunk —"

"I am not drunk."

Her head rocks. Jaw hangs. "I know. Yes. Because I know every part of your... how you do it. Happy and teasing. You drink and you smile and flirt. We make love and you drink. And you drink. Every waking minute you sip. You gurgle. You snurgle. Snurkle. Snoggle. Snoogle. Snurgle."

"You said that."

"You kill yourself with drink and every day I wonder what I will tell your baby."

All while she's talkin' I see that blackness crawlin' through her, selfishness writ in letters so big they roll across her skin. But I got to live with this woman, so I need to settle her down.

I'll talk sweet.

She'll be helpless.

"Hey there, you pretty likker beans. Pretty little beanstalk. You're a beanstalk. But your rack is better and better each day. And that's heart felt, not some bullshit to make you feel good."

Her eyes don't change. She's excited as she's capable.

"I've *stupid some done shit*, as the sayin' is, Tat, but I'm sorry. Let's move on. I know you got some feelin's in your head. Some ideas on the world I don't agree with. But you got a right to the bullshit in your noggin, and I got a right to mine, so let's call a truce and get to work on what needs worked on."

I watch my apology settle over her, almost like I said nothin' at all.

Squirrel back a ways run from a rotted stump to a beech trunk and skitter vertical. Off a good fifty yards, a hawk alights in a tree and his silhouette is stark next the sky. Five six earthworms tunnel under my feet, and over in the crick two trout bump uglies, or whatever way fish fuck, all afore Tat registers half a look of understandin' and offers me a gaze dead of all feelin' or emotion.

"You never said you are sorry."

"Accourse I — Let's see. What did I say? I thought I said, I'm sorry Tat, let's get it the fuck movin' on down the road, and all. Don't you recall me sayin' that?"

"Fine. I remember."

"All right. Good. Now we're on the same page. I was thinkin' earlier I kinda like this land. Somethin' 'bout this place got a pull to it. As I was walkin' I realize what it was. It's more like where I come from than any place I been since."

Tat smash a skeeter on her arm. Leaves blood. I look twice and it ain't a bite so much as a mosquito wound.

"You got that telephone?" Says I. "You want to call the number on that For Sale sign, there?"

"Why?"

I nod at the For Sale sign.

Tat fizzle-flash like that porcupine did and a tendril of black etch across her face, proof of the miserable and selfish thought she just put in motion. In that tiny moment she set herself agin me. In that tiny moment. Now her eyes go red.

I'm learnin' this shit. Yessir.

Tat smack her arm. "Mosquitoes are everywhere. And you never apologized to me."

Sit my new black jug on the truck bed and fathom it all.

This black hearted woman look into my eyes and lie, knowin' I spot the deception as the words tumble off her tongue.

Only stupidity can further inform a man in possession of the facts.

My explainin' work's done.

"Grab the phone, Tathiana. C'mon."

She smack her arm and wasn't even a skeeter there. It was just the first that give her the idea. She so slow and dumb I watch the brainwaves pop and splash where she put the whole notion together. I saw all that, kinda in another sense, a way of sight I just now discover. Like seein' words made of atoms. Maybe the porcupine didn't have the thinkin' horsepower to put off the charge, and I was blind to it. But I see Tat's thinkin' in the same dimension I see the black crawlin' on her face, like a transparency set in light from behind.

Tat say, "How many times did you say, *we don't shit where we eat*. How many times did you say *we strike and move?*" Tat climb out from under the tarp with wild eyes pointing back toward it, help make her point. "We have work to do here. Whoever did that to Carpenter. We can't settle here. We have killing to do."

As the mother of my future son look in my eyes with her mouth clamped shut, I see her thoughts like blue 'lectric over a grid, and see the words shoot out her like a cannon.

I can't live with him anywhere. God! How did I let this happen? His baby is going to be a monster.

Her words arrive without a voice, without the syllables even. It's the meanin' come through and make me bite my lip.

I got two minds, like the detective under cover got to live the criminal life while clutchin' the thread tetherin' him to the land of the good. I got this black shine in me resonatin' with the dark side, and I got to stay long enough to put this county right.

But Tat's words show me I'm 'bout to lose somethin' dear for it, and the honest-to-my-Maker truth is, this curse with the snakes under the skin keeps up, I'll put a stop to it with a bullet.

"Tat, please. Turn off your head a minute so I can get through. I can clear the land and be done with all the evil here in one swell foop."

"And no one will discover it was you?"

"Most likely not."

"Most likely."

"Shit. They's other things goin' on needs investigatin'. I can't say what all, just yet. I don't know. The fella responsible for that Carpenter dog is tangled in a bunch more shit, too. But we take him out without uprootin' the evil in the land, it'll be another man and another dog next week." Look back at Tat. Her face quit crawlin' for the minute. "So how 'bout it, Skinny Bean? You want to make that telephone call for me?"

Standin' now, Tat pull the phone from her back pocket and press it. She pass it to me.

Woman comes on and I close my eyes. See blotches of light but mostly black.

"McClellan's."

"Hey. You got that land down there for sale by the crick."

"Hello? Uh... Who's calling, please?"

That black in my mindscape tell me all I need and I open the eyes.

"Put yer man on. Please."

"Excuse me?"

"You got the land for sale, down by the crick."

"My husband will need to talk to you." Voice muffles. "He's rude."

"Hello?"

Close my eyes and watch.

"Hey, y'all got land down by the crick for sale."

"Wait a minute. Didn't we just talk? Are you the one who stopped by this morning and bought my son's old truck? Alden?"

Light pops. Shoots from one side my mind to the other and back. Then bounce off the top, or what goes for north.

"Indeed," says I, watchin' the fireworks and wonderin' what it mean. Get the sense I let too much time slip. "Yeah, that's me."

"You want to buy the land too? I didn't even tell him yet."

"What's yer ask?"

"Well, here's the thing. The land is in a trust for my son, but I got wind of this financial strategy —"

"Hold on. You're puttin' the horse ahead of the cart and we don't even know we're goin' for a ride, yet. So, let's put the cart back up in front the horse. What's your ask on the land? All I need, right now."

"It might not be for sale. I put the sign up, figuring I'd have time to talk it over with my son when he comes home. Which should be tomorrow. And the other thing is that it's a two-acre plot, but not even close to square. It's a tetra-hedra-trapezoid or something. It's cut out of the four corners of adjacent properties, and the goal was to make it a square. But they cut off the corner of each plot wrong, on account the same surveyor worked it out, and must have been on drugs or something. I'm not kidding about that."

"The land's a swastika?"

"No, no, nothing like that. The main borders are kind of square, but each corner's got a jagged bump for fifty feet where the surveyor was off. No one figured it out until ten years later."

"So, this land that maybe is and maybe ain't for sale. What's the ask, if it is?"

"I had five thousand in mind. Can I get your number and —"

"Your son's in tomorrow?"

"Expected tomorrow. Late."

"Fair enough."

I give back the phone to Tat and she press the red button.

Sound like total bullshit, that story. Get the corners wrong you get the line wrong. Way he said it, you'd get a smaller square, not some tetra nonsense. He was stallin', is what my regular self thinks on it.

But the part of me was watchin' the light while he talk, that part say the man ain't all bad, and what part of him is, ain't got the mental aptitude to give me any trouble. And I hear words smooth like water over round stones. *It's not a big deal. When people don't know people, they get touchy. Buying a man's vehicle and driving off isn't like becoming his neighbor.*

"Or pluckin' his daughter," says I, seein' the point.

A man needs details before he can know his mind. You know that.

And surely I do. The voice is calm and assured, and put me in the mind of country folk, tryin' they best to be decent, and confused why evil exist at all.

Look the sky and though it ain't dumpin' water on us right now, they ain't a touch of blue anywhere. It's all shades of black. But I got a sudden mind to do somethin' and got to get it knocked out.

I grab that first rock off the trunk and wonder how Tat lift it. Hold it at the gut and spin, open the arms and that gets it five feet. Good enough. Part the tarp falls and Stinky Joe scoot out from under.

Other side, other rock, same deal. I grab the tarp and fold it back.

Joe's scooted out and Carpenter's layin' there, pure ass dead.

Open the trunk, pull up my shirt, remove my belt. Pack that baby with 25 more coin and fill both my front pockets outta abundant caution. If it was real trouble with Tat I'd consider movin' all the gold to the truck, but she got that baby in her belly and I'd rather lose it all than have her raise my boy without the means.

I close the trunk.

"So, that's that," Tat say.

"It ain't nothin' else."

CHAPTER FIFTEEN

Me in the truck bed, got the bed mat out and the sleep sack on top. Tat's tarp is stretched proper above, with stakes and lines and not rocks marrin' the paint. Boots off, pickin' jam out the toes, poppin' joints. I got a steady flow of chirpy, low-caliber farts, one every five minute or so, kinda keep me in a pleasant mind. Drink black shine. Life's good, far as the bodily situation's concerned.

But each time I close the eyes very long I see the black was in Tat's face, and hear her thoughts, and I watch her go 'bout her business. Seein' her lookin' so beautiful and *claimed* — that's *my* son makin' her belly change — after learnin' her thoughts all I'd like to do is hurt her, and I don't know the source of the sentiment, as it's not the one I feel.

It's the one I think most loud.

All I seen her think is true, what I heard. Accourse I stink and fart and fuck and grumble and drink.

But I provide and I'd die takin' care of her and absolutely for my boy. Absolutely.

Plus, I'm fightin' a war for the Universe, on the side of good.

Bears mentionin'.

Snurgle of black shine. Put the jug down and close the eyes a long, long, minute and it feel like goin' someplace else, dreamy and light, nappin' on a cloud.

I'm up there a good bit.

And from the heights I hear some words, like sometimes you'll be on the dome and hear people talkin' a half mile down the sidehill. Women most times, as the voices carry, and they use 'em more. But this noise is sharp and cruel, words jagged like cuttin' tools, and though I'm floatin' up above I got the pressure build up in the chest and brain, the blood gettin' hot, and it wake me.

Open the eyes.

Tat's lookin' at me. I ain't let the eye contact happen these last couple hour, as that's when the snakes swim under her skin.

I turn the eyes away.

"Who the fuck are you?" Tat say. "Baer was just here. Where is he now?"

She step away to where I look. Lean forward, peerin'. Try to get her eyes latched to mine, to see inside, and I won't let her, and I wonder why even as I do it.

"The hell you mean?"

Tat swing her gun arm and that draw my eye like she want. She got the Sig on me, dead center, and the look in her face ain't the one she use on Baer Creighton, or Alden Boone.

It's the one she keeps for men headed forward.

Tat's ten feet off and I feel Smith in my hand, don't know how long it been there, nor why I pulled.

Did I pull on her first? Head in the clouds?

Whose face she see on mine, make her ask?

I go off thinkin' and come back to find the rest of me, in my absence, start a fight.

That pressure in the chest, the anger's a real thing. Feel my nose drawin' up in a snarl and my eyes closin' to a mean squint, even while the part of me was sittin' and dreamin' in the clouds is still lookin' on, still seein' the scene unfold with me in it, a man possessed.

Tat's got the whole camp cleaned. Somehow while I was thinkin' and not seein'. Everything put away.

Tat point the Sig on my chest and step backwards.

"I'm puttin' Smith down, Tat. I don't know what the hell's goin' on. I don't. Where you goin?"

"Joe," Tat say, and open the front door.

Joe scoot with his ass low, even more affirmation that somehow while I was dancin' with sunbeams in the clouds my body was down here doin' somethin' else and set Tat on edge.

Joe hop in the Eldorado.

"I will help you," Tat say.

She shift into the vehicle sideways, keep the Sig pointed my way. Though as she enter the car she gimme the angle I could shoot her six times from the side if I want. I notice without the ambition to do it — but like it's the very thing I was after.

"Tat. Hold on. What I say to you? I don't recall what I said."

"I hope later you will."

Tat lean out the open door and swing her Sig level. I spot

that orange blast and DEATH is the only word I got time to think.

But that bullet shatter the jug to my side on the gate, and all that black shine splash and drip to the mud and soak my legs.

Tat's eyes is cold and black as swamp mud. Her mouth is flat and the whole of her face convey a level of disgust two orders of magnitude bigger'n I got for all mankind, and she got it aimed square at my forehead.

Like she knows that's where she need to point it.

I put my hands on my lap with Smith to the side.

Tat lower her arm and now a light cross her eye, a question, and her lips pucker like she wished she could blow a kiss and can't.

Tat guns the engine and the Eldorado throws rocks.

I'm alone with whoever the fuck I invited in my head, wants to speak on my behalf.

And like I don't got enough troubles, the new zippy flash I see afore people change direction, the black snakes of ugly selfish thinkin' I see crawlin' below the skin, now I got someone from the dark side sayin' words out my mouth I don't even hear.

Tat's gone and the gas fumes remind me how much as a boy I like to sniff exhaust.

CHAPTER SIXTEEN

Engine sound's gone.

Camp is me and the crick water gurglin' off the side. Water's backed up like the drain goes under the road is clogged. If water keep risin' like it is the International'll be takin' swimmin' lessons.

I suspect, what I saw on Tat's face, if I was to give chase, she'd find the fact sufficient to put a bullet in me.

Feel like a squatter, now. No woman.

A man bound to eat onion and baby dandelion to answer his need for sweetness.

But the good news is a lotta likker's held in the International's tailgate grooves, conceived apparently in full anticipation of wild assed women. Iaccoca took credit I bet.

Ain't hardly demeanin', me to fold down on elbows and lap likker like a dog. Dogs is good people. I get the shine cleaned up, what I can, plus some dust picked up off the backroads, and dump crick water from a plastic gallon jug to rinse what I can't, so the black don't stain the paint.

I ponder that altercation with Tat. Remember how it felt, bein' on the dome, light and airy, and hearin' the sounds from the sidehill.

Was how I perceived it unfold.

When a man's of two minds, where's the second go when the first is carryin' the water? Second's in the clouds where it's pretty, as that's the place all men's souls go when the butchery is done and they get a minute to wish they never was born to start.

So now I got to figure a way to know which me I am at any given time, the natural me, subject to the appeal of the walnut whiskey, wholesome as thrustin' hips or a drumbeat by the fire, blood in back the throat...

Or the good me, gone sneakin' deep into evil, layin' traps, makin' war on the dark side, riskin' my eternal soul on account I ain't yet figured the way back.

And on account I'm comfortable in dark places.

Which lead to a notion clear as a firebug at dusk on my nose: spend too much time with the walnut likker, I'm liable to make a bad kill.

I can feel it — like it matters that I feel it.

I think on that a long while and the likker from the tailgate gets to helpin' and I discover they's no way to anticipate what I'll do, no matter the precedent, even if I set it. Maybe get suspicious, next time my thoughts is in the clouds. Other'n that, I got to hope Tat stay away.

Any other day of my life I'd know myself and my mind and what I'd do. Any other day I'd have the final hill to defend, the sanctity of the will and my capacity to use it.

But swimmin' in walnut shine, the final hill may not be there. More I drink, I don't see hills at all. Just easygoin' shadows. Sometimes, thinkin', I don't know which me I am. I got half my mind cooked on shine and the other half plottin' how to cook the rest, now that Tat shot one my jugs.

Twist the neck and look. Her bullet went in the cab after it went through the green glass next my leg.

Half my shine's gone, and I got a bullet in the truck.

I ponder the jug I got left. Look into the trees and think on the land 'tween me and that Hardgrave house.

Swing my feet and slip off the tailgate. Plant heels in mud and stand starin' at Carpenter there on his mostly dry blanket, still dead.

I don't like seein' a dead dog and I don't like handlin' dead dogs, but I got one. Tat took what earth movin' tools we had in the Eldorado. I ain't diggin' with a stick, and I ain't leavin' my spot here next the For Sale sign, afore I finish my purpose in this wicked land.

Duck the head and glance, unsure if I retain the luxury of private thinkin'. But if the land heard, it don't show and the land ain't the problem anyway. It's just playin' host, and'll likely rejoice when I scourge it.

I scoop Carpenter in my arms and cross the dirt road, wade into the brush and fight some briars, keep on 'til the thicket next the road abates and it's big trees with little undergrowth a ways, and I carry that dead dog a couple hundred paces, so even a hot day'll need assistance from the wind if it want to stink up the homestead.

Rocks like on my side the road, on this other side too.

They's two next each other and I angle to 'em. Where they meet at bottom is like God took a sledge and busted the corners off, so they's plenty space to tuck Carpenter back in. Decent chance his bones'll set unmolested.

I don't have any special words so I look at him from a few paces, hands on my knees and the muscles in my back bunched like to form a knot. I get on my knees and crawl back in where I pushed his body and rectify what irks me and leave him restin' so his feet is wide apart, each one, and not close like some toilet paper smudge left him tied.

Only prayer I got:

Lord make His face to shine pure hell on the man did this. Make his punishment Biblical. And I prefer the Old Book.

If it's your will.

Amen.

Once I back away and turn, it's a good blank walk back the truck, speculatin' on how exactly that shine'll first taste when I wet my tongue.

But I walked that dog out a good ways and it's a good ways gettin' back, and time I look at my new International, I realize I traded my unborn son for a fuckin' truck.

Lost a dog.

Woman too.

I wish I recall what the hell I said, drove Tat away. I think on my boy Moxie, and how if I don't keep my mind right and get outta this mess it'll be like twenty-nine year ago: Ruth birthin' Mae and tellin' me to go build my own fam-damily and leave her be. And me lettin' cowardice and excuses turn me away.

I didn't know Mae was mine, but I coulda.

If I wasn't so afraid of the fuckin' liars.

They must be four hundred places I could go back in time and kick my own stupid ass.

This day's a precipice and the rest that follow will be misery.

Unless.

Put my hand on top the jug to steady it, and with only two thirds inside full, that'll be enough for maybe a couple days' work. Don't know the full cohort of evil in these parts, but I do know both my restin' and work preferences for alcohol consumption, and stretchin' that jug two week or worse...

Fuck me. Ain't happenin'.

But I get the preconviction. I know what I'm 'bout to find as sure as when I was in that house and the locus had me in the hutch in all but ten second after openin' the door.

I need that shine. It knows I'm of two minds and don't care.

The locus, whatever inhabits that Hardgrave house and the shine, it's a force akin the nonlocal, the ether. Come from the same place, made of the same stuff, or its absence.

Whichever is the one is the other, is all.

I'm set to dive thick in the middle of evil, baned with two new curses, encumbered by black skin-snakes and the porcupine skizzle-fizzle, plus the old red and electric, and all that'll let me keep my cool while I'm undercover standin' next the liars and cheats is the walnut whiskey. It won't tame the curse, just give me a different point of view on what a thing means.

Let me bide my time.

The locus sees all that and don't mind.

It thinks it'll win.

And that means the threat is real enough I can't risk the mission on account of pride, or me bein' unwillin' to consume the walnut whiskey outta fear. I ain't a pussy. I'll drink as much of that likker as serves my Maker.

Yessir.

All that's left is to find more, and I suspect that old fella that put his face in the smoke at the Hardgrave house up there, he'll tell me where I'll find it.

I check Smith.

Dusk now, and I still ain't slept but what I did on the road 'tween the white lines. That black jug pulls me, and I take a pull back. Keep the poison in my mouth a long while, savorin' the walnut taste as the alcohol vapors float up in the sinus. Rub the tongue agin the teeth, polish off some grime. Whole mouth feel clean. Another swallow.

Another.

All right.

Hell yeah.

I rest the jug in the cab for safe keepin' and lock up. Look about, wonder when I last left a camp and it didn't have Tat in it.

I walk off mindful her betrayal, and I'm a hundred yards deep in the trees afore I realize I either got to cross the highway or walk through the water in the pipe under the bridge. Wonder if that's backed up too. Slow and lazy, savin' my energy on pure intuition, I cut right, follow the foot of the highway 'bout a half mile to the road, and from there walk like I'm official, not slinkin' about the way them FBI most wanted'll do.

Fuck the FBI, while it's on my mind to say it.

Ain't a few minute on the road and I wonder why I'm walkin' and not drivin', especially since I plan on carryin' likker back.

And here I can feel what the likker's doin'. Any ordinary day, it don't take but a nudge, I don't need hardly the tiniest conviction I'm wrong afore I quit what I'm doin' and seek a new angle on it. Fella can't be right if he knows he doin' wrong. But with that walnut whiskey in me, knowin' full well they's enough likker in the house to keep me snookered six weeks, and it'd be a damnsight easier to steal them jugs with a truck, I keep walkin', and don't turn back for the International.

Old dog learnin' a new trick. Learnin' to trust the premonition, when it insist on bein' trusted. I keep walkin' and as last time, spot the McCllellan place first, but turn to the Hardgrave drive right after, on account the Hardgrave house is tucked back in after a stretch of wood.

Toyota Tercel sit in the drive.

I shift toward the wood but get a steadyin' influence bolsterin' me, sayin' *Come and see what I have in store for you*, and I get a spark in the back of my mind like I ain't felt in forever, since one time Ruth and me was fightin' and fuckin', one of those horny angry days when we was kids. Spark say *it's okay to cut loose. Be wicked. The situation's contained; free yourself to the dark and be satisfied without bein' stained.*

The most tantalizin' advice ever heard by a human mind: no one'll know you did it.

Whoever make that offer... that fella know both the dark and the average man's soul.

He calculate my weakness and gimme his best, designed to hurry me closer, faster.

I stop. Give that dark spirit somethin' to ponder, let him know I ain't joined up entirely. I don't fuck on the first date.

And if he was all that, he'd a said somethin' 'bout her titties.

I stand on the drive lookin' past the Tercel into the side

kitchen window, seein' the candidate's sister, her back, as she's likely in front the stove yearnin' the days afore feminism.

I walk and think fast as my walnut whiskeyed brain'll do. I been the Destroyer so many time these past months it dawn on me walkin', this is just how it feels afore a killin'. The blood gets a pumpin' and the mind's not seein' things afore they happen so much as seein' the inevitable future while it ain't but a seed in the present.

I walk past the Tercel and glance inside. Sunglasses in the middle console, note pad, empty cardboard box on the back seat. Yard signs for the non-suicide candidate. A blue baby blanket. All I see.

At the steps I look up to the clonk of heels on wood, and she's there comin' up to the door. Apparently she slam a glass of wine down her throat on the way, and stand there with her mouth like an O, skinny glass upside down in her hand, eyes maybe turned over too, while some the vino spills down her windpipe and neck at the same time.

She knits her brows high. Spits. Swallows, mouth suckin' air. Half out her mind drunk, stooped, fist on chest and snortin', gigglin' and with her mouth open like a lake bass, she look about to faint.

She get control of her throat and stops gaggin' long enough to lean on the jamb and tilt her head like some girls do so you know she ain't just pretty, she puts out too.

Her legs fall out her skirt into cowgirl boots with pink flowers stitched in the sides. Her knees look like she don't pay 'em no mind, but I don't know exactly what she ought to do to make 'em better. Cover the fuckin' things up. Good thing is, I doubt I'll be lookin' at 'em very much.

'Less she folds 'em high.

I get one boot on the step and figure if that's what she wants, she'll back up and make a gap and let me through the door. But she just looks and smiles, maybe happy she ain't gaggin' for air. One more boot on the step as she straighten her neck, push her bangs back over her scalp and I take another step, and one more, and then on the porch turn sideways and invite myself in.

She stays in the doorway and I wish one of us was thicker so we'd smush. I give my back eight-inch clearance so my chest got none, an push agin hers one by one, so I can feel each sack a fat press oblong and roll next my chest, then slide and when I'm outta titties I'm inside the house and two thirds laid.

I smile at her like she smile at me.

"In Guatemala they got a sayin'."

"What's that?"

She lean her face closer to mine and I see her lashes is low on her eyes, so in her head it's maybe like she's seein' me through gauze.

Her lips pull apart and her tongue clicks, she got her mouth dry that quick. Need some lubrication.

"You're the man from the grocery."

Her nose touch mine and she back away quick, flirty and dangerous. Gaze like a hungry chisel, if they was such a thing.

Her jaw's wider with her smile so big, and that make her neck appear a little thin.

Wonder how it don't break on its own.

"What do they say in Guatemala?" says she.

"I'm gonna yodel or fuck, one. You got any preference?"

She's swingin' in for another pass at not kissin' me and stop to bob her head and grin stupid. Not sayin' she's stupid, just finds her dumb look pretty easy.

"Yodel," she says. "And if you're good…"

I draw the tongue over the front teeth 'til I got 'em slick, make a show a crossin' my leg over my nuts and twistin', though it don't hurt my nuts on account they's a good several inches lower. Seekin' my absolute highest register, and knowin' those luscious nippled orbs is a wink away from gettin' thoroughly enjoyed, I phrase it out:

"Yoda lay he hoo?"

She punch me. Kiss me, and like my crotch was on fire she's pattin' and tuggin'. Slurp kissin' on my face, half off my mouth, tongue jabbin my cheek and suckin' while she do, like to stretch a welt from my jaw to the knot of my shoulder.

Can't help imagine if I could get her on her knees.

She's close enough the college age her fingers remember how to unbutton a man's shirt backwards with one hand while crank startin' him with the other. Ambidextrous, for a drunk girl.

"Mercy that tickles. Hey! Like to keep that nipple."

She go south. Ten second. Twenty.

"Hey! Shit! Leave some skin. C'mon, now I ain't playin'."

I pull away and take her hand.

"The kitchen," she say. "Butter."

"Don't you want to know why I'm here? Or how I know what here is? Or what I'm lookin' for?"

"Yeah! You said." She think. "You said were an angel from Guatemala."

"I said all that."

"Yeah. That was you." She squint. "Right?"

I watch her throat while she talk, in that narrow little pretty tiny neck of hers. The lines is thin. And if I was to measure, I bet my right hand'd get two thirds 'round.

CHAPTER SEVENTEEN

Shit of it is I got a ninety-eight percent chub already, and from prior situations like this I suspect we wouldn't need any more words to commence the rawest, fingernail dragginest scrog in Pennsylvania history. But every time she move her neck I see a new fragility, and the walnut part of me seeds ideas in the black part of the mind, way in back, long past where the eyeballs beam the world inside. Back in the shadows I see both my hands on her neck, and like a sickness, I don't even hunger for them tits.

A sickness.

But while I'm in it the sickness is just and make sense. I got that awful black smoke in the mind like it was whirlin' 'round the room, that old bastard with the beard and the bullshit, sings the song of industry and might. I know it ain't right, neglect a woman with an appetite, but her sex and her hunger is almost — in this shitty evil corner the mind, make so much sense while I'm in it — almost like her desire for me is the reason I ought to grab her neck quick, while my hands is on her shoulders and she won't know I'm puttin' her down 'til she's lookin' up wonderin' why.

Do it.

Close my eyes. Squint like to crush the sockets and close the cave, collapse the vision.

She got both hands deep in my drawers and her face is like a nerdy girl with a empty wine bottle and some alone time.

But that old fuckin' locus is in my head grinnin' his encouragement. Mountain of a man, tall as a tornado, got a beard like Heston playin' Moses. His whole self is made of smoke but sculpted the way some men'll drag on a pipe and blow a perfect three four rings, keep they shape while they float off. He's crowded out the other black shit in the black shit part of my brain, and now this fucker's musclin' in on the light part, and I wonder how it is I thought I'd take him on and come out breathin'. Or at all.

It's so suffocatin' in the dark, it's clear the Almighty's condemned it. And if I had any sense, I wouldn't be in it.

But He sent me.

Didn't He? Send me?

Maker, you better get word to my hands afore that monster get 'em to do somethin' I can't stop.

And like the woman hear, her shoulders drop a wee bit.

And the locus hear me too and his teeth glow.

I see how you think. I know just the cure for what ails you. Imagine water can only be hot.

"Yeah, fuck you," says I, in my head, on account they's still a prayer I find my senses and screw her, not do her. No sense alarmin' the woman.

She pop up and kiss my mouth and while I let her she

move to my nose, and put the whole thing in her mouth. Teeth. Tongue probe a nostril. Randy ass woman. One hand on my ass and the other dropped down my drawers and cuppin' my jewels.

"Easy. Them's sensitive, yet."

She loose my nose and I can't even wipe it to the shoulder. Transfixed like I'm in a coma. Her knees buckle and she let her hands drag down my chest while she squat in front. Works the button as she's already conquered the buckle and zipper.

Imagine you're the One who made water, but all you get is hot.

"Fuck you, spectre. You're the cussed locus. Forsaken as a motherfucker. And you know it."

Shhhhh. Ain't you something?

I feel that fucker in my mind, flippin' couches, tossin' drawers, bustin' plates.

Hmm. I see.

"The fuck you do."

The fuck I don't.... Baer Creighton! Look at you. Trying to run. Wading in blood.

"I'm stuck. Is all."

And who told you to let the blood?

"You know it."

Yes, I do.

"On account a people like you. And you know why."

More than you.

She's got my tool in her mouth and workin' it like a champ. Farther back my eyes roll the closer that bearded locus come. He already took most my mind and now he's pressin' out.

Lean.

"What?"

Lean. She wants you to grab her tits. I want to feel them in your hands.

"How 'bout maybe you rally some common decency? You and me'll settle square after I pass her out. How 'bout that, sport?"

Sport. Chum. Blud.

"Ain't yer fuckin' blood. I'm here to kill you."

I know. But you can't. Only One can, and He won't.

Hold my tongue. Locus gimme pause.

Woman remind me of the Electrolux Ma had, back when I could fit it.

Imagine you created water and can only drink it hot. You created it but can't know all of it. That doesn't make sense.

"Almighty do anything He choose."

He can't contradict himself.

"Fuck you."

Perfect is a prison.

"Fuck you."

That word carries a lot of significance with you. Go ahead. Fuck her. I want her too. It's been days.

"How 'bout you fuck yourself?" Think a second. "And maybe keep talkin' on the water. I don't exactly ken ye."

Wait? Been days? He's had her? Who with? Whose dick —

How can He know His full creation? He can't without your eyes. He can only kill for good. How does He even know there is evil? He understands it. Conceives it. But He doesn't feel it without your hands because he can't participate without you.

He smile. Waitin' on me. I don't give him shit.

Us. Without one of Us. He can kill in virtue but never in evil. Without you. Or me. Our kind. He can't feel hatred and love the feeling unless it's through your heart. Or see it, without your eyes to see through. He doesn't know it unless he knows it through the condemned. Why do you think he builds so many condemned? If he's good and has the choice and the foreknowledge? Why create the condemned, at all?

"You're fulla shit, spectre. You are *the* shit-fullinest —"

Do the math. He has the power to do all. See all. Be all. Future and past are one. He knew what you would be from beginning to end because he understands entireties of the real and you understand slivers of illusions. Even steeped in Truth He chose you.

"For what?"

To work for me, on my behalf.

Wanna giggle at the fucker. "You tell the Almighty I'll need it in writin', preferably on that wall right there. You get that, I'll still think you're fulla shit."

I nod at the wall half expectin' to see the Hand of God, and that bump my mind and instead I look at my grocery store woman and marvel at her mastery of her gag reflex. I close my eyes and the whole vision's sparks and murals made a swimmin' lights and toothy shadows givin' chase. And she's suckin' like she want to keep the last four inch as a souvenir when she's done.

Think! I've been here a long time. How?

"How what?"

I'm not hiding. He knows my home. How does He permit me?

"I don't know why."

Not why. How?

"How."

How is He capable? Of course, there's a reason for the Why. But you won't know Him until you conceive of the how.

I'm blank as I don't know what. Got the likker in me, woman's mouth slobbin', demon — maybe satan his own self — in my head.

I'm only a man. Ain't built for it.

"Maybe the Almighty quit his permission, and sent me to —"

You? Wonderful. Let's explore that, Baer Creighton. Poke around here a bit. Oh, there it is. Spent your whole life hating yourself, cursed with the ability to perceive the liar's heart, and knowing there was nothing you could do to stop seeing it. You hate the lie — You — the biggest liar you've ever known. You shove that knowledge so deep you don't even remember, and it drives you about like a madman, pretending honor. The biggest liar of all, and you know it. But you're not honest enough to confess it. No, Baer Creighton. You're not man enough to put me down. Not equipped. You'd have to admit you love killing. And it wouldn't matter if you did because your Maker needs me.

"Then why we talkin'?"

Think, Baer. Why would your Maker send you to me, if not to kill me?

Maybe if I open my eyes, I won't see him.

I open 'em and nothin' change. The same black smoke, demon eyes, barely see the room about me and the woman half exasperated at my wiltin' mess.

"You're doin' fine, woman. Keep on. Say? You got a name?"

She grunt somethin'.

I'll tell you why, Baer. Because you are going to work for me.

Back inside my head — "You never said how He's capable. You said why. And the fuck I am."

You are cleverer than you look capable of being.

"Quit stallin'."

The how is the easiest part. We're One.

"Bullshit."

You thought it yourself before arriving. I saw that. We're the same stuff. Different intent. He's hot. I'm cold. He's him. I'm you. All the same stuff.

Spectre's face is like an old man sittin' atop a whirlin' cloud of a body. The Good Book did say the great satan was a pretentious asshole and schooled in the art of trickery.

CHAPTER EIGHTEEN

"Fuck you, spectre. I got your number."

How do you say it these days? You got shit.

I want to say somethin' big and blustery, but feel like a child got caught misbehavin', and just now learnin' they's no way out but the truth. So inside I squirm and reach for any mean words handy and come up with a mighty sermon:

"Fuck. Well, I do think I'll manage to kill you one day."

You won't because you don't yet understand you can't. I'm not made of the stuff you have power over, Baer. I'm woven into the fabric. I'm your father as much as He is.

"We'll see."

You. You'll see. Baer, this isnt' a defeat. You'll do your best work for me.

Ain't easy, got a war with three fronts in the brain. Kitchen smell like lathered woman. Demon wants me to choke her to death and the Almighty got the tiny voice, like a whisper, sayin' *it's time to go.* I ease back to a sober corner for a full thought rendered in clarity and understand none of this altercation means anything right now, it was all information, reconnaissance. This wasn't the moment for action but the moment for learnin', and long as I don't commit any unforgivable stupidities while I'm here, I won't lose any ground. I'll escape with some knowledge.

But I don't hear that I'm escapin' with the purpose of returnin' and sendin' this demon back to hell.

Which set me to wonderin', in that tiny space of a sane moment, why am I here at all?

I come for more likker but was under the spell when I launch the first step, and each one after kept me hypnotized in the purpose. But in this crystal clear moment I see the Almighty stretch a path...

"Hold on Missy. Back off."

I unseat her hands from my waist and unsteady, she drop on her rear, which she got half naked while I was elsewhere. Pristine ass on the kitchen floor. Somethin' 'bout the white parts of a bikini tan moves me. But she look like the cartoon with the eyeballs wound different directions. Somehow, she manage to get half her chest out her blouse too, and it look like the kitchen's got the ingredients all laid out for a proper fornication. But I got the bigger sense of my surroundin's, the ambush I let myself get drawn into, and while I got a flicker of sanity I turn to the wall and knock my forehead agin it, one more, one more, one more, hard! That spectre's lodged inside and won't cut me loose, so the Spirit of the One who sent me show me the path out like footsteps stretched for me to walk in, like that verse when Paul said we was made for good works. The footprints is gold and light, and me with my dick out hard and sloppy, my back and loin tense and pleadin', I put one foot on top the golden step on the floor. Dizzy. That spectre's in the head and the Almighty give me the knowledge I won't escape the evil 'til I escape the land. He got still more advice for me: don't got to be such a numbnuts with the shine, give the great satan such an advantage. So, I put the next foot in the next gold print and the next.

"Where are you going?" she say.

Specter snarl at me.

You pussy.

"Fuck you."

"That was kind of the point," she say.

"Not you. The spectre."

"Oh great. Another flake. What is it about this house?"

One more gold footstep, one more. I'm at the door lookin' out and those gold feet lead out the porch and down the steps. Cut right toward the lake I can't see but for the moon off the ripples. Disappear down over the slope but come back close the water anglin' rightward.

"Hey?"

She shakin' her head, suddenly soberer. "What?"

"You fuck that spectre? That what you mean?"

Her face wrinkle like a bulldog.

"I apologize. Musta been a different — I don't exactly know how to say it."

"What spectre? What are you talking about? You're freaking out. The last man I brought here freaked out. And the one before that."

Didn't know they was so many so close. How close? She didn't say and that's an opportunity for me to not ask and not know, and thereby not feel like I just went streakin' through the syphilis factory.

"You don't know the spectre?"

"I don't know."

"C'mere."

Hold out my hand.

"C'mere."

She at my side. Skirt up. Chest hid. I'm still half out my drawers and she grab aholt.

Cuff her hand. "Mind yourself, Lyndon."

"You call your johnson Lyndon?"

"All accounts, he was a big dick too. Now pay attention. Look."

I point at the first gold footprint on the floor, waverin' and glowin' like a fire seen through someone's window afar. Then the second and third, top of the step. I point out each one, "there and there and there. You see 'em?"

"Do I see what?"

"Gold footprints."

"What are you on? Seriously, what are you on? Because I need an escape. I feel like I'm coming apart."

I step to the porch, close the door.

Her wrist in my hand, I pull her along. Down the steps, 'round the right and down the slope. Each step is like it's mine already; as my foot meets the earth the gold step gets in under it, like to marry it with divine purpose and propel it onward.

I got to see where the footsteps take me.

"Hey! Where are you taking me — my wrist hurts. Stop!"

"What?"

"You're hurting my wrist."

"Oh."

I loose her. "You don't see it I guess, but these gold footsteps circle 'round and stop right over there."

I point.

It's dark but they's a good size moon somewhere behind the clouds and the light's good enough she faces where I point.

"That's where the walnut tree was," she say. "Over there. You can see the, you know. I can't think of the word."

"A tree."

"No. The hole."

"You couldn't recall the word *hole*?"

I think of three jokes that don't advance my purpose, so I mute 'em.

"I happen to be mildly intoxicated. And it's more of a pit, not a hole. Want me to blow you? I'll do it right here."

I think of walnut whiskey. The poison. The black in it, and the original walnut stain, come from the rind.

"What walnut tree?"

"This again. I can't get away from it. Didn't I tell you the story? You saw the movie, right? We talked about this. Can't a girl just get laid? Look at me! I'm *hot*. Why won't anyone fuck me?"

"You talk 'bout a lot of things. Refresh me on the story."

She touch my unit. "I don't understand why you want me to stop, but it'd sure help if you put your meat away."

"Unh. Pardon."

I fix myself. The zipper slide and it's the only sound in the dark.

"Okay," she say. Exhale. "No sex. Fine."

"You can do it."

"Okay. If you say so."

"Be strong."

"I'll survive."

"Refresh me on that story."

CHAPTER NINETEEN

"There used to be a walnut tree over there. The first settlers here killed Indians and hung them on the limbs. Part by part."

"What you mean, part by part."

"Limbs on limbs."

"Oh."

Cruelty itself carries the pain after so many years. I think it and hurt.

"The movie said there's as many as six women buried over there, where the tree used to be. Three of Angus Hardgrave's wives, and three other girls that disappeared from town and no one ever guessed what happened. Plus, all the Indians no one kept track of."

"No one ever dug 'em up to see?"

"Some folks talked about it back when the movie came out. It was going to be a big thing — its own documentary. I think they were trying to get 48 Hours interested. But each time the men came to start, they'd get sick, or not show up at all. Then the main guy who was pushing for it died, and he wasn't anyone big anyway, just some media guy for the movie studio. And by then perfect little Matthew got his Oscar and everybody decided to forget about Walnut, Pennsylvania."

"He a pretty shitty actor or what? Why you got such a beef?"

"No. He's amazing. I'd fuck him 'til Friday. No, really. I would. But he opened every closet in my family's house for the world to see, and we have a couple skeletons in every corner."

"What you sayin'? Him wantin' to dig the graves was all movie promotion?"

"Matthew never said anything about it. You know Hollywood. They have swarms of marketing minions. There isn't anything real in any of it. Or any of them. They tell stories. They don't live stories. The rest of us get to."

"Nah. They're fuckups too. They live plenty. Don't you read the material you sell in the checkout line?"

I'm lookin' out at must be another thirty footprints leadin' that a way, but while she's talkin' the wavery gold does the porcupine skizzle fizzle, flash like the television signal's busted by the clouds and disappear altogether.

My feelin' of divine inspiration followin' the gold feet do the skizzle fizzle too. I was warm a second ago and now got a chill, like I'm in the land of the men I sent forward but someone else did the sendin', and the souls know they was took unjust, so the land stays cold as rage.

I take her hand in mine and though my stones still ache for release, this woman ain't the one, ain't mine and I don't want her.

Hear the water ripple at the lake edge.

That spectre set the trap and like as not knows the Good Book better'n I do and can seed thoughts such as I heard on that Paul line on the good works, which I suppose the apostle intended for the folks of Ephesus more'n me.

You'll work for me...

Spectre sound weak like half his power is what I give him — and since the Almighty show me the corner in my head where I can have a clear unmolested thought, I got most my mind shut to him.

I'm out from under the spell and bein' drunk ain't enough reason to fall back in under it.

But it's my fault this woman wants sex. I can't hardly rev her up all the way and never put her in gear. That ain't right to her, and even if I don't want to fill both hands with nippled splendor to slake my own lust, I feel duty-bound, after a manner, to slake hers on account I'm the one got her hormones riled.

Right is right.

I take her hand soft in mine, say, "I got a place down a ways where its quiet and we can finish what you started."

"You're not some psycho are you?"

"*Eccentric* carries most the same load."

"Hmm. Should I wander off with an eccentric man from Guatemala?"

It's a damn crazy thing: bein' honest I'd like to tell her goin' off in the woods with some fella she don't know after he said the shit I said, that's a dumb proposition for any woman. But I'm the exception, and I doubt she'd much care what I said if I also said I'd poke her, so I don't say nothin' else. Just pull her by the pinky 'til she's next me, walkin' up the slope to the drive, and her car, and leadin' to the road and the turn back toward camp.

Time we get there it's a good fifteen minutes and I got a sweat in the lower back and butt. Mind percolatin' and turnin' over the events. The dead dog, the truck, Tat runnin' off, the black shine, the demon looks like an old man swirlin' like smoke in my head, jawin' back. The black snakes under Tat's face. The porcupine skizzle fizzle, how he flash and go staticky like a TV lost the signal. The gold footprints laid out like crumbs to the very locus itself, the hole in the ground where all the sufferin' of untold injuns and wimmin of old was dumped, so it could fester or ferment into the cloud of injustice that hang over the whole county like them black clouds that dumped rain like a train crash on the sidewalk.

"You know what," she say, standin' in the heavy dark down in the hemlock, with only our night eyes to see. "I don't want to do this anymore."

"By this you mean me."

"Yeah. You're a little weird."

"Well, that's true. And on my side, you come across like —"

"Like what?"

They's no reason to hurt the girl and tell her the only way I'd feel safe after stickin' her would be to amputate the part that did the stickin', and we don't ponder shit like that. At all.

"I'm glad you said that," says I. "You're beautiful as all get out, and if all you want is a romp, I'm sure you'll find one. Just don't bring your next man to the house, and you'll be fine."

"The house?"

"Yep."

"You're not telling me you believe any of that?"

"Don't you?"

Weird, talkin' to a woman in dark so deep I can't see her face, but just imagine it from afore. Plain and pretty. And to her credit I never thought of her knees agin, after first seein' 'em, 'til now when I'm tryin' to think of what's wrong with her. Most women you don't got to think so much.

"I used to believe all of it," she say. "The house used to make me feel weird. And something happened to me, where the tree was. But nothing's happened in so long…"

"What happen?"

"Just your normal ghost stuff. I felt cold. Felt like hands were touching me. That sort of thing. Active imagination, right?"

"And then they did a movie and you saw the exploitation. Of the story."

"Yeah. So no, I don't believe it anymore."

I shrug in the dark half outta sadness for her. But it's dark.

"Here, let me walk you home."

"I know the way."

"You know the way?"

"I grew up here."

"Right."

"So long, Guatemala."

"Say, you never did say your name."

She's already walkin', and it's dark enough I don't know if that's her toothy smile glowin' back a second, or just some more bullshit shimmerin' in my mind.

CHAPTER TWENTY

I GET IN BACK THE TRUCK AND SET THE JUG OF BLACK SHINE on the ground where with any luck a sasquatch'll come by and steal it. This seem like a place that believes.

Get settled in the truck bed and I dream the woman with no name. I'm crackin' her hips with mine and it's like a jungle for the sex and steam and heat in the truck cab. Each time I hit it she burps. She's wore out. Draped half out n' off the seat, them massive piles a perfect vanilla puddin' splayed like they's drunk too. I love bikini tans, and I want the whole cussed world to know.

I rear back high and give the moon a good howl:

"AWOOOOOOOOOOOOOOOOOWWWWah — yup."

"What! Shit!"

Some animal wanderin' too close skitters.

"AWOOOOOOOOOOOOOOOOOWWWWah — yup."

"What? What! What! What the fuck? The-the-the-FUCK?"

She's beatin' my arm. Buckin' hips. Shriekin'. I got nothin' to hang onto and she launch me to the dashboard. It's like I was fuckin' satan in the form of a woman. My calf from the punji stab wound feel like I drop a brick on it and I thump my mess off the gear shifter, and shit if I don't think johnson Lyndon's busted in half.

Piss me off.

She slide off the seat — this is a dream, now, y' recall — land outside on her back and the whole world's dream-squishy, like you see good what you see, but that might only be a sliver as wide as the woman's pie. The whole backdrop is woods at night with some sorta purple phosphorescent haze 'round whatever shit I'm lookin'. And dead square center is this woman's sex, wide open and raw while her butt hits and her legs flop, a split second takes maybe a hundred years in philosophy-time to settle flat and square and all the ripples to play out in the mind of a man like me.

What a perplexing thing is a woman's sex.

I seen deer gizzy. Bear gizzy. Squirrel and rabbit. All manner a gizzy — but try just once and see a woman the same cold way.

Can't be done.

Want it like to kill for it. Many do. The way you baby it. And do your brutal damndest — as she insist — to smack it down 'til it won't bounce back off the mattress. All floatin' on titties, tongues and kisses. And as much as it confuse him — as he's made for nothin' else so much as chasin' down pussy — once a man find the woman he was intended, he'll give up his life in a second for that pie, and for the progeny that come from it. He'll bust his ass day in and out, if he's a man, a real man, to make sure his woman and kids is looked after, no matter what. He'll sweat for 'em and if it's the only way, a regular everyday man'll summon the courage to bleed for 'em.

Thinkin' that, I watch this crazy non-suicide brother's sister's snatch and all I want is to beg the Almighty to grant me one more visit with Tat so I can crawl on my belly and beg her forgiveness.

I'm a failed man in every regard.

Hell of a dream!

And neither am I sayin' this dream-woman's gizzy is unappealin', in the strict biological way a man is sometimes required to regard a woman.

She bounce. Bring the left leg hard across and catch me as I tumble out the truck after her, still holdin' broke johnson Lyndon in my hand.

"What the fuck is wrong with you! Go away! Get away! Stay back!"

She skitter off and leave me to the dream fog, and I open my eyes.

Already noddin'.

Most dreams is bullshit, I'll be the first to confess. But this one time I'll take a meanin' and assume it's the Almighty talkin' in a language I can understand. I know the carnal strain in me — and it seem the whole thing take the air of the Book of Job — was put in me by the Almighty and brought to a heady peak by the walnut likker and the non-suicide's sister.

She shoulda had a name so I'll give her one. The non-suicide brother's sister's name is Gretchen, 'til she tell me otherwise.

So, Gretchen was took over by the evil one to act as a lure — and if the whole trap was set by the two of 'em, even with the Almighty puttin' satan in his place and makin' him stop shittin' where he eats, they was together pullin' my strings, and not coordinatin' worth a shit.

Is the truth.

And that makes it like the Book of Job.

Anyway, the Almighty know the titties sometimes lure me off my logic. The lesson with this whole blueball fiasco was to be more mindful of how the evil one uses fine lookin' women...

Or any woman, is the truth.

I figure all that out comin' awake.

Sit in the truck with my back agin the rolled metal top of the bed and my head on the glass, 'til my head start slidin' back and pullin' my neck, and I got to straighten up and take accountability for myself.

It's cold — or I'm underdressed for bein' sweaty. The air's fulla bug noise, as they ain't yet bedded down.

I wonder on Tat. Where she's at. Who she's thinkin' of. Probly out at the club lookin' for a man to —

Nah. Way she left I imagine I screwed it up for all menfolk. Fine. If I can't have her, I want her a dyke.

Settle back in the sleep sack and don't get a wink 'til I wake from the deep, like gettin' drug out a sack of molasses.

CHAPTER TWENTY-ONE

EACH TIME I WAKE IT'S LIKE MY BRAIN'S IN A SOCK GETTIN' swung in a loop, kinda mushed on the right. Shortly after dawn while the woods is yet gray, I search a jug a water. Find none, so I pump enough crick water to fill the five-liter water bag come with the back pack and drop a pill to kill the Germadiea. Chlamydia, Ghiradella.

The Water Worms.

Drink enough I'm sick and lay down. By and by sleep come, and I wake agin with dull light pushin' my left eye. I get up enough to drop johnson Lyndon over the edge — ain't broke after all — and while I'm on my knees the pressure in the brain is mighty and cruel. After I start and stop three times I'm done, regardless, and let myself go easy back to the bag and foam mat. Close the eyes and though I can't sleep, I let the thoughts come and go easy, mostly uninterested, as the misery of the walnut whiskey hangover's more captivatin'.

Once my back and side hurt as much as my head, I find a

couple Goodies' Powders with the aspirin and caffeine. Four's a good start.

Fix coffee. Find a pack a bacon slipped out the grocery bag and under the seat.

Cook bacon. Eat bacon.

I got the water bag drunk to nothin' so I pump it full agin, and notice the crick water's comin' higher, and the sky never got blue and bright this mornin'. As I'm noticin' the humidity and stink of roiled water, and lookin' up expectin' rain, I catch a heavy drop on the center my forehead, feel like a small baseball.

Weather in west Pennsylvania seem to be gray with water comin' out, all the time.

By early afternoon I've thought on Gretchen enough to want another go at stickin' her, though it ain't likely. Woman put on a show like that and not get laid...

Bet I made her a dyke too — and that set off a new round of imaginations.

But each time I think on Tat and the news she gimme — I got a son comin' — I want to finish whatever the hell it is I think I need to finish here and see if I can't pick up Tat's trail.

I tell myself that, knowin' full well they's no way other'n luck I'll catch her scent if she don't want me sniffin' 'round. I just hope she seen a piece of my heart all the days we rode together. I been loyal in every fight and with her and me joined with a baby, I'll be loyal in love too.

Much as I can.

And I don't hedge 'cause I know johnson Lyndon so well.

I hedge 'cause I'm just startin' to learn I don't know the Almighty at all. He's a helluva lot bigger and more capable of everything He's capable of, and that include some of His Old Book ways.

I settle on the thought a long minute, 'til the Old Book and my headache is one.

That jug of walnut whiskey in the corner of the truck bed, lookin' at me, starts talkin' with words I can almost hear. But I don't get the sense this afternoon'll best be spent swimmin' that swamp. Like to bust that jug on a rock, but not knowin' what's in store, I best keep it.

Hard to make sense of all what happened in both the world 'round me and what I took in of it: the swirlin' smoke and demon. The satan.

I recall the gold footprints, how they cut from the porch and down over the hill. Was like a fella dipped his feet in gold paint and took a stroll 'til you get there, and the footprint move to meet the foot.

Gretchen said it was injuns murdered first, then a buncha women.

If I could drive that International to Chicago and visit Mags, I'd do it. She'd know if souls get trapped.

Everything else she tell me, I can't feel especially confident sayin' they *couldn't* be trapped. As most everything I ever thought was, ain't, on account most words ever spoke is lies.

And everything I thought couldn't be, is.

I ain't confident for good reason, and that very lack of confidence in the one inspire me in the other. If I'm so wary a this world, I oughta consider everything in it suspect. And if everything that couldn't be, is, then all my dreams as a boy of findin' a right and just world is almost in my lap, ready to live. The place of all good things is there, real, here.

I just got to be good enough to see it and seein' it I'll be able to step in it.

And there I'll just live in it. Easy's that. Livin' in the perfect world's as easy as bein' perfect.

All a fella got to do is quit bein' himself — and none of his other natural selves — to find it.

But that's on account they's nothin' at all I'm confident in sayin' can't be.

I'm little, next the mountain.

Weak under the storm.

Split by the mirror.

I think on livin' good, simple and pure and it'd be a damn fine rest. But if it didn't heal me deep, all the way down, I'd pick a fight. Wake some people up. Just my nature, and it's a good thing, as I got a fight ahead.

I ate all the bacon but left the grease. Got no bread, nothin'.

But I know a grocery, sells it.

I'd wink if I could see myself do it. But those thoughts is for later, if night calls agin, and I come runnin'.

For now I got a fight to grok.

Is the locus a man? Or a swarm of injun warriors, a pocket a souls forgot and left to stew on this side, while history's moved on and no one'll ever mourn 'em enough to intervene and send 'em home?

Maybe they ain't evil so much as trapped by it.

And maybe they yet serve the Maker's purpose, in misery.

I think and wonder if them souls and me 'd find kinship if we could locate a common tongue or sign to speak our common hurts. And from that, the things make us smile.

Good chance all the evil in the tree hole, and maybe elsewhere, is just pent-up hurt felt by the trapped dead.

My enemy ain't the soldier and I'll spare him if I can. It's the general needs his head shot.

Whatever souls is in the tree, they ain't the spectre. I can see it now and I can see why I'm stuck here.

I got to learn how to kill that old fuckin' ghost was in my head.

Somethin' tell me the time I do that I'll avenge whoever tied and left that Yank dog Carpenter to suffer and die.

Tat's gone and I got to get movin'.

Best thing's go back to the house where I bought the truck and see the son from Congress. Ask questions 'bout the land. And on the way see what I see of the Hardgrave non-suicide's house, and maybe Gretchen in the window. But keep on for the McClellan joint, as I suspect the son and wife and, well, all 'em, is pure goat fuckin' evil.

Can't have a family live equal close to the locus that make one man off himself and his sister a nose chewin' sexpot, and not be tainted with one kind of crazy or another.

Walkin' off, I look back at the International. No dog. No woman. I got a fine truck, a Smith & Wesson Model 29 and britches on my ass. That'll do.

Jug's hid behint the back tire.

I'd take the woods, but I doubt the crick's backed off any, and if I can't cross under the highway in the concrete drain, I'd rather take the road. Don't seem like a hell of a lotta risk of the lawman comin' through. This place don't know law.

But it will.

Left at the Y, 'round the bend, up the first hill and look at the second. Ahead a bit, black marks from some hotrod layin' rubber. Posi traction.

On farther up six eight turkey buzzards flap off with wings so heavy I can hear 'em. Must be a deer to gather so many carrion birds. It's a likely place to hit deer; corn fields up ahead, forest on the other side, and bein' cut in a channel the roadbanks is high. And it'd be hard to see very far ahead, comin' up over the —

I stop and my guts roll.

CHAPTER TWENTY-TWO

Air taste like blood. Feel my feet pressin' socks and rubber, asphalt, the earth.

That ain't a deer hit by a F-150.

It's a Gretchen — though it ain't right to call her by a made-up name, now she's dead. Accourse, it's more right now 'n when she was alive, but then it didn't matter.

After the interstate bridge is skid marks, wasn't there yesterday. Meanin' whoever hit her slam the brakes after and not afore.

I peer at those marks from where I stand and lookin' close, the skids is from stoppin' one way and spinnin' out the other.

He went back to hit her agin.

Still stopped, I cut a foot for the woods right next me, but halt.

Someone was to come along while I'm haulin' ass up the bank, and they's a dead woman up there, he may not tell the law, but he'd damn sure tell the barber. And this is the kinda place where a barber might soak in one good story and spit it back out a thousand times. Short order, whole town know to keep an eye out.

Then the cop he didn't tell 'll get wind anyway and call it a clue.

Best thing I can do is walk like a fella walk when he ain't murdered someone.

Try and remember; oughtta come easy, as I didn't murder Gret — the non-suicide's sister. Who I guess don't look much like a suicide neither. But seein' her as I cut wide and skitter my feet quick — stomach rollin' — half her chest out her blouse —

I got to throw up a minute. Just fuckin' dandy, leavin' spore next the body — so I hold that yak in my throat and once the reflex quit swaller the bile and bacon back down.

— and seein' her there like that, chest half out and she's stuck in a mat of blood pooled on the macadam, I get her confused with the dream-memory girl fallin' out my truck, flashin' gizzy. Some blood's dried but the rest is still shiny like glue. Her face is knocked so her expression don't make sense: eyes and brows soft like I imagine she'd look if she said she loved fawns and foals. And her jaw's busted half sideways. Blood out the ear hole.

Rest of her, the angles ain't right, so it hurts to look, and the vision don't stop when the eyes turn away.

I get past and point the face straight ahead and keep the arms swingin' and the lungs pushin' air. Blinkin'.

Woman had enemies. Passin' out them *Fuck the Government* stickers. Middle finger for Congress. Woo Hoo for free speech! This is America!

Pretty fuckin' retarded. May's well say I breathe air. Woo

hoo. Yippety fuck. Who care? Everybody think, *fuck the government*, if they think, and they ain't in it. None but a pussy want another man tell him what to do.

So why take the risk? Them politicians love the power and they love the ass kissin' comes with it. Lord 'emselves 'bove the men and women put 'em in office and a tiny one-two them politicians engage in criminal behavior.

I know. Say it ain't so.

Which is to say whoever help her brother not suicide himself mighta helped her.

That's it but it ain't.

I got the tingle-brain goin' on, and I think on the path laid out dry between the raindrops.

I look to the Hardgrave house like I thought I'd be lookin' for Gretchen in the window.

"She's dead," says I.

Hearin' words'll sometimes make 'em ring true.

Pass right by and keep the arms swingin' for the speed. Don't hardly notice a half mile pass. Cross the McClellan grass and right up the steps and I'm rappin' wood.

And while I'm hearin' foot stomps inside the house headed the door, I'm seein' Gretchen back at the house afore last night went silly. Back when she was just a horny girl feelin' her oats and mashin' the floor. Rootin' and stompin'. Suckin' my nose. Suckin' everything. I'm seein' her engage on me like she did, but from a good ten feet away, out the window.

Tat see that?

Her man possessed by the devil and ready to consummate his stupidity with the whore of Babylon?

Tat put a dent in the Eldorado's back quarter panel.

What if she ain't left these parts?

What'd she do to the bumper last night?

But fast as the thought flashes 'cross the mind, the one chasin's even spookier: I best verify the condition of my own bumper on the International, 'fore I speculate too far on what evil Tat mighta done with the Cadillac.

Jesus said that.

I don't know what I did. Don't recall squat, 'cept it didn't end happy.

I was sober when I started and if I murdered that girl, it'll stain my soul forever. Not like these evil fucks, killin' them's a credit.

Standin' on the McClellan porch and fist a-poundin', I catch a vision and follow 'long in my mind like I start walkin' back the way to her house from camp, up the slope, 'round the bend, up the hill. The dream vision ain't real. I know it but I don't. And when she's at the foot of the steepest hill of the three, the vision change. I climb inside the International and follow with my headlights off, crawlin' 'til I can barely see her, and I gun the engine and clutch one two three up the hill. Right afore the bridge as I'm 'bout to run her down, I turn on the lamps and the beams cut her as I take the final bend and she turn and raise her hand, and her eyes look like her scalp is ripped back, makin' one-inch sockets into two.

Door pull open. McClellan's already got his mouth open and say, "Hello, Mr. — Shit... I forgot your name."

"I thought a second you gimme a new one."

He smiles flat, look me up and down. Eyes don't got the same friendly dance as when he was sellin' a truck. Men don't hide intent from they eyes worth a shit. But he don't look mad or mean so much as decided and puffed on himself.

Fucker gimme the boss-man look, is what he did.

"What?" Says I.

"Hello? *What?* You knocked on my door. We have to talk but, shit. Can I help you with something?"

"Not lookin' like that."

"I don't understand."

Now his face is back normal. I don't get the red eyes nor the juice, nor the black lines and the skizzle fizzle. I don't receive a signal at all to help me understand this man, but I do understand, regardless, from that first boss-man look.

Every animal on this planet with swingin' nuts knows what an inferior man is, in its own kind. And it know if it is or it ain't one.

You can offend a man, get him confused with the inferior.

CHAPTER TWENTY-THREE

"Fuck you."

"Excuse me? You come knock on my door to say fuck you? Who the exact fuck do you think you are?"

"The exact fuck? That ain't your privilege."

"Baer Creighton," says he, a touch proud.

"Fuck."

"Yeah, fuck. I've known you from day one."

"Guess my picture's up all over."

His smile's weak like that ain't the truth but it'll help 'im if I believe it. My whole life I been seein' the lies and it's this one — which maybe ain't even untrue, exactly — push me over the edge.

Says I:

"I'm callin' on you to be a virtuous man. You know that ain't how you know my name."

He turn his head half way like to go inside the house but instead the look satisfy him to close the door, him on the porch with me. He ain't armed. No red eyes. No juice. No skizzle fizzle. No black veins. All my tools says he's shootin' straight and stayin' the course.

But he ain't.

"I saw the special they did a couple weeks back," he say. "FBI's most wanted. You're a dead ringer for yourself. You ought to do something about that."

No juice. No red. The man speaks his words like a taunt. I'm missin' somethin'.

"You're asking the wrong question, Baer."

That's what I was missin'. I think.

"You ought to be asking how I knew to expect you. How I made sure to make your acquaintance."

"Make a lotta sense. Good questions."

"I bet. Sit on the porch with me a minute while we talk."

"I'll stand."

"Good. Do it over here so I don't have to turn my neck. Because I'm sitting."

True to his word he drop his ass to a wicker sofa with big pillow cushions with a lady bug pattern.

"Come over, like I said."

I cross the deck, see how the paint ain't cracked nor dull and they's no bug shit or cobwebs on the sidin' nor windows. Fella's a little up tight. He got a picture window to the living room a little behind him, to the side, so I can see the wall and end table at an angle. Don't give away much. Dog bed with no dog next the patio couch he's decoratin'.

That sofa with the ladybug cushions do look comfortable.

I nod at a chair and he nod back. I sit in a home style Adirondack, cut from some soft wood with a hatchet and fashioned with no other tool but an auger.

Stained walnut.

From the look.

I put hands on knees. Feel awkward sittin' low with my legs high and wide, and I pull back my hands only to see I'm cuppin' my nuts and got to move 'em agin. I ain't one to cup my nuts in front a stranger. Can't say I do it at all; I'm perplexed as to why I would now. All while this son of a bitch is smilin' at me with that boss-man look agin. That *I own you* look says: *you'll do as I bid and if you don't I'll beat you down.*

"We back to that shit agin."

He smile and the look go poof.

"I don't know what you're talking about," McClellan say.

"Look here. I know you're a weak man, so I'm givin' you the chance. I challenge you to be honorable and not use tricks of perception. If you got a square argument, you can make it and know I got a square mind. We'll come to some accord."

He hold my look, hard.

"But you keep after the deceit and trickery, that tell me the exact opposite. Any man lies to another is a man confused by his lack of worth. Weak, but unwillin' to accept the natural station due the undeserving. So he use deception to make him equal the man earned his place by value and virtue. I know your kind. World's swimmin' in pussified men, each calculatin' as fuckin' politician. *Don't think* you'll use the lie on me and not suffer the rightful consequence of a lie meetin' truth. And if that ain't you — if I got it all wrong and you ain't a weak assed liar, then stand on the truth of your words and be as tall as you are and no taller. You think on that long as you need to know what to say next. I'll do somethin', one word or the other."

He sit a long minute with his eyes lookin' 'bout a foot to my left, over the rail and out the cornfield, other side the road.

I want to turn and see, but don't.

The house is on the same side the road as the Hardgrave place. I look through McClellan's picture window and the side window on the other wall and spot the back corner of the Hardgrave house. To the right, which I can't see on account the wall, and down over the slope is the hole in the ground where satan's golden footprints led. Calculatin' the angles in my head I suspect that locus is exactly behind McClellan's noggin right now, and I wonder if he got a plume of black smoke trailin' circles in his brain, look like an old demon, tellin' him what to do.

I'm back in the midst of it, but this time sober with a headache.

He stomp twice, tilt his head. "Two, one…"

The door open: his old woman.

"Yes?"

"Bring iced tea. And sugar, as our guest is a suther-enner."

She go away. My speech a minute ago got me focused and riled so I ain't thinkin' on my nuts no more, 'cept now. But the steam keep me afloat while McClellan's regained his aggravatin' self. I brace agin whatever the devil just told him to say.

"Like I said a minute ago. You asked the wrong question. That's why you couldn't see my deception."

"You said that."

"You see red eyes. You feel electricity. Correct?"

"Who the fuck —"

"There you go again. Wrong question."

"What's the right question?"

"It learns."

"One more smartass word and I'll end this conversation a

way you won't appreciate. You will, but it'll be in the nonlocal, so —"

"Baer, you need the question that gets to the real point: how did I know to expect you? A deeper question, and better: How is it that you and I — with opposing masters — are talking at all?"

I sit. Wish I had that ice tea. Maybe help the headache and the sugar give me a little pep.

Says I, "In all candor, I don't favor people who ask questions just so they can spout the answer. It's dishonest."

"Bah. You should know. The one who helps me has already explained most everything to you."

"The sphincter. Specter."

He frown. "What's it matter, the name we give him? He has goals. Your boss has goals. They coordinate when they need to. You asked for the square truth so here it is. You heard all this last night. You and I have been tasked to work together. You did your first job last night, but in the future, you'll be taking instructions from me."

Little black worm — two, three, six slither from in under his jaw like they was hatched out the very vocal cords that utter the lie. He's talkin' and I'm thinkin' on what he said a few seconds back, how I see the red eyes and feel the juice.

Didn't mention the crawly face snakes nor the porcupine skizzle fizzle.

"Takin' orders from you? He didn't say that. He said a lotta things but not —"

"He's telling you now!"

I mum up. The man's animated by the evil and I suspect the only thing keepin' him out my head is the lack of walnut whiskey. Glad I kept some for the final battle.

And glad I don't got it in me right now.

I need a happy thought to buoy me for the battle, and the eternal self offer up a memory that always make me smile: one time when I was young, I broke a fella's nose after he called a girl a slut and she gimme me a blowjob for it. Always fond to recall.

McClellan lean in his sofa cushion and take my measure. "We have more work for you."

"Speak a little plainer."

"You did a good job with Gretchen."

My asshole puckers. Him usin' the name I made up.

He keeps on:

"Maybe went a little farther than you had to with the sex, but no real harm. She was a beautiful woman. Easy to understand a man needing to indulge. Especially the sort of men we get, you know. Assigned."

"I don't follow."

"I think you do."

How many times can I say *fuck* at this man?

McClellan look back and forth like he suspect a sniper in the cornfield. "Anyhow, you're working for us. Your next assignment is a reporter we're having a little trouble with. But the catch is that you're going to have even more trouble with her, based on what you did last night with Gretchen. You know."

"I don't want to know what you saw. But I kinda gotta ask."

"I didn't see any of it."

"You just take the word of the spectre."

"Yes. In all things. I have a master like you."

"Not quite."

"Exactly, quite, but you're too stupid to realize it. Momma

brought you up in Sunday School. I bet you grew up memorizing Bible verses. Sing hymns to yourself in the shower, so you don't play with yourself."

"Never did that. I'm tired of you. What about this reporter?"

"Your second job."

"You mean you want me to kill her? Or him?"

"That was easy."

"What else am I gonna say? I'll consult with the One" — *she's gonna bring me walnut whiskey in the iced tea* — "what? Lost my train a thought. I'll get on bended knee and if things ain't right I'll make 'em. Is all."

Sometimes my thinkin' comes unbid. But welcome, as I need to avoid any and all kerfuffles 'til after I get a look at the grill on the International.

Says I, "Somebody oughtta call the police or somethin', on that body."

"Gretchen," says McClellan.

The door opens and Mrs. Boss-man rest a cold glass in my hand, and I sit it on the porch floor. She give the other to her old man and watch my eyes too long goin' back to the door. She stand there.

"Aren't you going to drink it?"

I give the poison a sniff and smile at her. Odd she got no red in her eyes, and I got no juice. But the black snake on her face's big enough to punch.

Ready to call her shit out, I think agin. Just 'cause I know the truth don't mean I owe it to the liars. Better let 'em think they understand fully what power the Almighty gimme.

"I bet it's delicious," says I, "but I already gotta piss."

Return the glass to the floor.

"You said the girl's name is Gretchen," says I, thinkin' she mighta said it while we wasn't pokin'.

He nod.

Woman let out her breath and the screen door slam.

"We're going to let her age in place."

"I don't follow."

"I know you don't. Listen, I don't know too much about what makes you tick. I don't care. You guys come to us when we need you. It's part of the deal. Another part of the deal is you don't ask for information. You don't need any, but the name. That's how it works."

"Part of what deal?"

"The deal."

"I don't recall a deal."

"Not your deal. The deal we have —"

"Which?"

He keep his mouth tight, like it let him down.

"I thought as much. You're fulla shit half the time and stand on lies and treachery the rest. Tell me what I need on this reporter. What's the story?"

"No story. Just a name."

I stand. Walk to the step.

"Baer Creighton. Kind of rolls off the tongue."

"Your meanin'?"

"This house and grounds are covered in cameras."

"You had any nuts, that'd be a threat."

He smile broad. "Don't be mistaken. It's a clear threat. You do as you're told, and you do fine. We finish a few jobs together and you move on. After that, we're enemies. But for now, our masters think there's merit in you working for us. So, you're going to."

I look the old pudgy fuck up'n down while he sit on his ladybug cushions. Belly out like he got a demon growin' in his girl parts. Wouldn't even need Smith. I could walk over there and snap his neck in four seconds, as the hangover has me feelin' scrappy this mornin'. Watch the pee stain his lavender shorts and have his old woman meet him on the other side afore he's done messin' himself.

But I won't.

A year into my escapades I seen 'nough the evil to know it got aholt this clan, so much it ain't the man and woman but the house and hills. The dirt and grass. And if I send these two forward right now, they'll not be missed here nor celebrated there. Just regular ass evil. Better tools of the trade, no doubt, but all evil's ordinary, as all it do is destruct.

But that vision come over me on the porch… seein' Gretchen turn as the headlights land on her, eyeballs in terror…

If these fuckers put the spell on me and I did that I'll murder each six times for it. But 'til I know what I done I can't do no further.

"Mister McClellan, I can promise you when my Maker cuts me loose of this operation, you'll be the first to know. But I can reason same as you and the Almighty wouldn't gimme the signals I'm gettin' without a divine reason, and if I do somethin' you say, it ain't got shit to do with you sayin' it, but Him."

He hold my look and unstick his tongue from the roof of his mouth so it pop, and that's all he got to say.

"Yeah, well like I said once or twice: fuck you. Gimme the reporter's name."

"Heidi — the little bitch's name is Heidi but she's a natural born liar, and her first instinct was to use her middle name.

Known her since she was two feet tall." I watch. McClellan grab the armrest and wrestle to his feet. "You'll like her too, just like you did Gretchen."

I get the sense my admiration of the female anatomy figures strong in his thinkin' and schemin'.

Says I, "Easy on the eyes."

"Red hair, short like the lesbians keep it these days. Tits like softballs — she goes by her second name — Preston. Thinks she's clever: works for the paper and calls herself Press."

"You soft on the woman."

"You will be too, unless you steel yourself to her charms. What you did with Gretchen was all right if you were only supposed to be a man. But you're supposed to be cut from a different cloth."

"So why you demons think she got to go?"

"That isn't yours to know. Goes back to what we were saying a few minutes ago."

"I'll ask her."

"Before you put her down?"

I watch him.

"Fine. She had a part in the Levi Hardgrave's suicide. She wrote a story for us."

"You closin' the loop."

"No. She'd be useful if she'd take instructions. But now she's nosing around for another story. She wrote the exposé that drove a congressional candidate to suicide. Her story ran all over the country. I saw on the internet they ran it in Israel. Imagine that. She makes fifteen grand a year working for a paper with a circulation of forty thousand, and we got her on three Sunday talk shows in one day. The gall."

"She writin' you up next?"

"Nothing like that. You have enough to do your job — and I've told you more than any other of your kind who's worked for us."

"Only reason I ain't ask for more is lies is no use, past the point they describe the liar."

I push off the porch and on the first step grab the rail and turn back. "You remember what I said. When the Almighty lets me off the hook and we're through, you're gonna know quick."

"Do something stupid and you'll find you don't understand anything about hell, at all."

"Right. Well, go fuck yourself and have a good day."

CHAPTER TWENTY-FOUR

Knowin' what I'll see if I walk back the way I come make me want a different path.

When I put the push on McClellan his head was froze lookin' forward and I speculate the devil was pullin' strings from behind, and I trace the line back to where the gold footprints led, down over the slope and back to where all them dead Indians and women's buried. That's where I'm goin'.

Off the step I cut right.

"Hey?"

I'm in front the porch, crossin' the yard.

"Where you going?"

Shake my head. The devil's man's heard enough words from me. I'll do my best to keep any more to myself, 'til I send him forward. 'Cause one thing's sure.

This fucker's goin' forward.

But I stop and make myself a liar. Turn.

"You got that dog bed up there empty and the woman askin' me on day one if I seen him."

McClellan nods slow, brows high. He grins.

"And a minute back you said the question was how you knew to expect me, and to guarantee we meet."

He add a nod to his smile. A teacher viewin' enlightenment.

"I thought a while it was your boy, the congress critter. You look too busted down to walk ten feet in the wood, let alone carryin' a dog. And no woman's that wicked. Then your bitch brought me the spiked tea and I thought it might be her. But it dawn on me she's an order taker and you're a natural born son of satan, and I bet you could jump over this rail and swing a club at my head if you want."

Ain't grinnin' so much, now.

"You tied that dog and left him. Dog's name was Carpenter."

His brows close in tight while he figger somethin' new.

"How'd you know his name?"

"You told me. Plus he told my other dog and my other dog told me too."

McClellan nod slow and I float him the bird crossin' the last of his front porch.

"You look pleased with yourself," says he.

I stop so I can still see him and while the last parts add up in my head my floatin' finger lose some buoyancy.

"You couldn't carry him in the wood, though. You took 'im on a leash."

He shake his head and the realization hit me like a fist.

"You said heel and Carpenter follow you in. I'll be a son of a — I'm murderin' you. It's gonna happen, McClellan. It's gonna fuckin' happen."

It's like watchin' the television while the storm come in and the signal go weak. McClellan's face and body, his whole damn self, confusion and course correction under way. Got the skizzle fizzle while he think which direction to play me.

He can go to hell.

I cut to the woods and the slope that lead to the lake and tree. Got a mind I might go back and cut that fucker to his knees right now. He led a capable dog into the woods and tie him just to send me lookin'. Just to make sure we meet.

My eyes is wet and I miss a root. Land on hands and knees and stay there. Half down the hill to the lake, I can smell it in the dead air. See water glint here and there through the leaves. Maybe a good swim'd clear the noggin. No, not this noggin. I got so much hate in me I could murder Pennsylvania and be done with it.

But how'd he know I'd wind up campin' at that one spot?

I rest my head on the ground and hope some the evil thoughts fart out my ass.

The great deceiver told him... but how'd that lyin' fuck know? Unless the great Almighty give him the info?

The satan ain't Godhead. Ain't the mover and shaker. Can't set the future. He just distort the real and send our worst after us, callin' us to be worse still. So if the satan knew and told McClellan where I'd be and how to snag me, it was the Almighty told him first.

My stomach knots and I couldn't fart to save my life. All this wicked thinkin' in my head leave me a sputterin' fool in the leaves.

I seen it my whole life but never let myself think it wide open: good and evil ain't opposite forces so much as differin' vantages on the same thing. The world I know ain't real and the one I don't can't be seen.

They's no other way: the One who made me was in on it. The One who made me was there when McClellan tied Carpenter's feet. I can't riddle it. Just like he was there with Job when all his women, kids and animals died. The One who made virtue made evil too and is just as handy with one as the other.

He was there when my mother swung a shotgun by the barrel and didn't save her. That maybe ain't wicked and cruel and evil from His hill, but it sure as fuck is from mine.

I rise to my feet but with the wind sucked out my lungs my knees got no strength for walkin'. I crumble back to 'em. I hate my knees and I hate the earth they land on. I hate these God damned trees and this God damned land. These God damned people.

Yankees.

Suther enners.

Foreigners.

And me.

And…

"You fucker!" says I, not sure if I say it to Him or me. Or both. "You FUCKER."

CHAPTER TWENTY-FIVE

THE WOODS IS STILL AND EVEN THE RED SQUIRREL SHUT UP. Now ain't the time to antagonize ole Baer.

After I press what loose water's in my head out my eyes and spend a melancholy minute wonderin' where my precious Tat is, and my precious Moxie in her belly, I find my gumption and draw my forehead out the leaves and plant my ass next a beech, and sit with my arms on roots, wide and high.

Forehead's wet. Ass is wet. Elbows and knees.

This fuckin' state. Rain never quits.

I got a sliver view of the lake. Out beyond is fuzzy distance. Skeeter next my face. I swat. Miss.

"I won't serve evil."

The Almighty don't say a word, per his usual.

"You hear me? I'm on my own. I ain't so ambidextrous as you. So, keep your curse. You can keep the new shit too. Them fuckin' snakes. That skizzle fizzle. I don't want none of it!"

Get myself worked up agin. Slap the tree.

"How the hell you think to solve evil with me out here doin' more of it? You said to take the plank out my eye. You said I'm the problem and I am. That's your whole book right there. Both your fuckin' books. I'm the problem. I know it. You save me. I get it. But I need fresh savin' every day. And if I'm the problem how come you give me more tools to be a bigger problem? I say it again. I won't serve evil."

"No, but evil serves you, Baer. It sure serves you."

I roll. Hop to feet and swing Smith so fast McClellan stumbles back, catch a rock and land on his ass.

"I thought by now you would have understood," says he.

"Understood what?"

Silas plants both hands at his sides so he don't flop over. "Baer, you haven't been serving your maker. You've been serving mine."

Keep the sights 'tween his smug eyes and let my ears wander, hear if any other's around.

"Think, Baer. Answer your own question. How does all your killing rid the world of evil? Your killing is good, and everyone else's is bad? Yours is honorable, but the other hit man who thinks his killing is honorable too, you believe he's wrong? Your code is good; his bad?"

"How you'd get so close and me not hear?"

I look back up the way he come and it ain't twenty feet I cross in the woods. Rest is lawn. And most them twenty feet's on a dirt path.

"You were crying, Baer. Sobbing. Man can't hear when he's sobbing. I'm embarrassed for you."

"I never kill a man from personal shame but they's always a first."

"Funny, given the conversation. Who would that serve?"

"Me. And maybe it's about time."

"You do what you feel you need to do."

I fire Smith and McClellan's head is mist and echoes. He ain't toppled half over and I lope past, get blood on my leg from the fountain.

Up the hill.

I'm gonna murder that fuckin' woman 'fore my senses get me. Cross the lawn. She heard the shot and if she got any brains, she'll have a gun on me. Be a blessin' if she'd use it.

Not givin' a right fuck I march straight the way I came, cross the front porch. She's peerin' out the door and spot my pistol, duck back inside. I come 'round and take the steps two at a time. Stomp like a man refusin' to run. She lock the screen and leave the main door open. I rip off the handle. Kick out the bottom glass. Punch the screen. Yank the door free and inside it's all nice cabinets and store-bought flower smells. Piss me off even more. Pick your own fuckin' flowers. You live in the country.

She's so evil and dumb she trip on the staircase corner headed 'round for the laundry room.

Summer dress on an old woman. The mean part of me want to shoot her varicose veins first, same as I'd lance a boil or pop a zit.

Now she's on her side, shakin' and mutterin' gibberish. Her son. Her husband. The true king. The secret knowledge. She try crawlin' off but I get aside her and drop her with a gentle boot to the hip.

She farts.

Screams — tryin' to take my eardrums out, I guess.

A boot to the teeth solves that.

In the mind I hear some the words I'd ordinarily say, if this was a ordinary operation.

If I had my usual eloquence and steady bearing, I'd tell her she's a hardboiled cunt but the Almighty love her anyway, and she'll soon suffer the ultimate torment relivin' every moment of her evil and feel real pain through the eyes of the ones she hurt. And 'cause I'm a softie I'd mention after her due and fair sufferin', the Almighty'll restore her, and she'll be wiser from the hurt, and in the end it'll all work for the good.

It's a good thing, me bein' strong enough to launch her redemption.

But I keep mum, as all I'm thinkin's murder.

She live next the evil, soak it in, so even if she was born two counties over she spent enough time here she's a daughter of the deceiver, and while I got a clear mind and the overwhelming judiciousness and righteousness and fury, I hold back the boot that want to kick her in the face one more time, and fire a bullet through her right cheekbone instead.

Step back and take in the full living room. Look all over, as I can't hear shit from my ears ringin'.

She's dead at the doorway to the laundry room and if I had time I might do a quick wash. Got blood on the leg. I give the pit a sniff and ponder. But if I did a wash I'd just stand here naked lookin' at her. And I got shit to do anyway, if I ever want to see Tat agin, and raise a boy.

If.

I don't know if I'm the one either need.

Silas McClellan said the day I met him his son the congress critter'd be here on the weekend. Tomorrow. Or this evenin' dependin' on how early he get in off the airplane.

When he does, I'll be waitin'.

Maybe even drag his old man up the hill with his brain spread out on the lawn just so this little congress monster knows what to expect when Smith comes lookin'.

Been a long time since I give a fuck for the dead I make, once they's made. These two is no different 'cept if I feel anything it's a spark of reprieve — from myself. A spark 't says I don't need another to carry the weight of the sin I was yoked to when he made me.

He made both me and the sin and it's good of him to carry the fruit of it, so long as I confess, I'm a worthless piece of shit to start with.

Ain't that love?

Don't mind me, Lord, I'm just talkin' to myself.

And if that forsakes my soul then I'll keep doin' like what I done 'til I can't do no more. And when it's done it's done. And when I'm gone, I'll meet the next life with the same clear eyes as this one.

Eternity can fuck itself if it's more of this.

I back out the door and look up and down the road and as usual they ain't a car in the county.

So, I cross back in front the porch and head to old man McClellan.

It's the spark of God in a man that make his life worth respectin'. Without, he's nothin' but animal. Same with the ladies.

I shoot McClellan's stupid ass twice more in case that floatin' fuck satan has a rescue in mind. Better yet I fish out my knife. Drop to my knees with one on his cheek and hack off his head. It ain't desecration as they was nothin' holy in this man's life, nothin' available for redeemin'.

I tote McClellan's noggin by the gray roots to the lake and damn near bust my ankle drop kickin' it twenty feet out.

From the ker plunk, the water's shallow.

I don't wait to see if evil floats as I ain't drownin' witches. I turn left and pass below the Hardgrave house in the pit that used to be a walnut where they bury the souls time forgot. Keep on through the orchard and avoid the non-suicide's house altogether. Back through the woods and at the interstate the water's backed up like I thought it would be, so I climb the grade, wait for a pause and trot across both lanes while the traffic's thin.

All this time I been doin' the Almighty's will, I been protected from the evil with the talents.

But the killin' don't fit...

Comin' down the second grade after the interstate I fall on my ass damn close to where the porcupine did the skizzle fizzle.

Sittin' there I wonder on the anti-Biblical stupidity of it. The Almighty made words come from an ass so I wouldn't put it past him.

But would he electrocute a boy and leave the job undone, so it give him the curse? If so, I wonder if the so-called well-spring of truth and existence and energy and matter has a clue what a moral is.

Did I ever serve the Almighty? Even once?

My hate for the lie burns so hot I can't bear myself. Can't bear my thinkin'. And for the first moment in my sorry life, after all the pain of Ruth and the pain of Fred and every other pain that wrung me dry of love, I want it over.

I'm a murderer, not a father.

The rain clouds, all the dark gray, that sticky air, the

climate of evil — the sky of West PA opens and a beam come down like Michelle Smith in school said was how souls go to heaven.

I see the answer so big in glorious light, the question give me shame.

I never done a good thing in my life.

Eyes closed. Trucks and cars zip past above on the highway and some the wind come down the slope. They can't see me. It's thirty feet at a grade.

Part of me is a boy in the country, decidin' I'm the only one to trust. Part of me is a gray hair in the desert, a wanderin' fool. Or prophet. How you know?

And in the middle is a stone-cold self-deceived murderer.

I recall the porcupine and how he fade in and out like a bad tv signal.

I wish I could skip to the end of my story.

At the International I see I didn't hit Gretchen. Bumper's good.

Wish I'd a stole a Twinkie from the McClellan kitchen. Stomach's a pit.

Ain't that the way of biology? No matter the philosophical heights a fella's brain'll ascend, he can count on his belly to keep him grounded in the natural.

My eyes is wet like I been cryin' more but I ain't.

Sky's opened up blue all the way from one side to the other, what I can see through the cover, and the sun make the leaves and land crisp and edgy, like the whole scene got an artist to go over it, make it pop.

Air smells better.

My little camp here at the crick ain't but a fire circle and truck. If I drive off without knowin' how fate'll have me return... What then?

This spot's the only bridge 'tween me and Tat and my boy. I leave for good, how'll she find me? How'll I find her?

This fuckin' melancholy. Like to murder it.

While the dirt is yet mud, I scrape with a rock:

LOVE YOU GIRL

I'm a dumb cock. Whatever hell I made it's mine to live.

Well, shit. There's a virtuous thought; one good thing I always do is sleep in the bed I made.

I drag my boot over the words in the mud.

Fuck all this shit. I'm gonna kill what yet needs killed and get the hell outta here.

CHAPTER TWENTY-SIX

"Heidi."

She turn.

"Who are you?"

"You wrote the story on Hardgrave."

"That's not my name."

"From the tattoo on your cleavage there I'm bettin' I got the right gal."

Blank stare.

"Don't get me wrong. It's pretty."

"Who are you?"

"I got information."

"I'm not Heidi."

"Preston."

"Press." Big ass fake smile and she mean me to see it. "The Hardgrave story's as dead as he is. Make it quick; I'm getting coffee."

She look at Starbucks, case I don't pace her logic.

"This info's for a new story. How a reporter*ette* made up some shit for the devil and got a man killed. And his sister."

Now her eyes ain't pretty and without the eyes a-glowin' that quill and ink jar on her tit ain't so glorious neither.

"Let's go inside. The weather says it's going to rain."

"What's the blue sky say?"

"Wait a minute. Have we met?" says she. "You look familiar."

"The ladies say I put 'em in the mind of that skinny ass actor."

"No, that's not it. You have my interest. Who's the reporter?"

"You."

She move her mouth around without sayin' any words. She find a couple.

"What is this? Are you hitting on me?"

"You better get your mind in the fuckin' game. I know what you did, and you got but one chance to fix it."

"Wait here and I'll be right back with my coffee."

"Let's sit in the shade. Now."

She look me up and down. Spot the blood on my leg. Eyes go squirrelly. I had any brains I'd a washed my britches in the crick, but her fear's handy.

Says I, "We're in the open and I ain't what I look, exactly. But you start some nonsense, I'll make sure the world'll know what I know, and that'll include your part in makin' four people dead."

"The story keeps getting bigger. What do you want?"

"You're gonna tell me what I need to know. Then I'm gonna tell you what you don't, far 's I can. You're gonna write up a big new story and get your bigtime job. Or I'll kill you, one"

Her jaw fall and she turn a half circle. There on the cement, broad daylight, middle a Dubois right next the Starbucks, a man just threaten her life.

"I'll give you the full ballyhoo, accourse."

"Wait a minute. I know you. I saw you on that FBI special."

"You got a lotta options but only two outcomes: you live or die. Wanna walk to the bench and sit a minute? Or die? Here on the concrete."

"I'm not accustomed to being threatened."

"I don't repeat myself, so your customs is safe."

"I'll walk to the bench."

"Thought you might."

I watch and she watch, like a power move, holdin' back when she said she'd go. Like a big fuck you.

Lotta big fuck yous in Pennsylvania.

I keep her look and kinda fall inta them saucy pupils a hers. Swim in a pool of warm motor oil, or somethin'. It's a dreamy bath and from the vantage swimmin' in her eyes I could dive right 'tween them mounds.

But while I'm enjoyin' myself, deep in back the mind, I give her the chilliest mountain stare I got, so much I want to shiver.

"Move, damn you."

She nod twice real fast and scoot with motivation. Her jiggles'd ordinarily be the sort to capture the imagination but all I want is my work done. She turn on the sidewalk and I cross the grass. We meet and sit.

"Whose blood?"

I twist my leg. "That's Silas McClellan."

She turn away. Back to me. "What do you want?"

"Who approach you with the story?"

She raise her brow at my leg.

"Silas."

"What he say?"

"He said that his son was Congressman McClellan, and he had information about his opponent in the election."

"Dirt on Levi Hardgrave."

"Sure. Right. Everything's dirt, or it isn't a story. I'd already written five hundred words about the barn fire. There wasn't much of a story to tell."

"Gimme the high points."

"Well... like I said, there really wasn't much of a story. Levi's barn burned down. He was there and I wasn't, so —"

"Why would you've been there?"

"All I'm saying is —"

Red eyes. Juice.

"Bullshit. Stop. Why would you've been there?"

"Levi Hardgrave and I..."

"Shit."

"Yeah. It was complicated."

"Y'all was fuckin'. What? You got a better word?"

"Our relationship was complicated."

"Sure. Why not."

"One more thing. We were engaged."

"True love."

"Are you kidding? — Oh God. You're serious? Hell, no."

Now I'm the one with eyebrows workin' a sovereign choreography.

"He was going to be a congressman. It was a sure thing. My

ticket to the inside. You know how hard it is to become the Washington, D.C. correspondent for any news organization? Let alone the big ones? And you know what happens to the careers of the journalists who prove themselves in Washington?"

"You get a bag of jellybeans. What happen next?"

"I got a better proposal."

Tiny bit a puke come up my throat.

"What?" She say. "You threaten my life and turn into a wimp when I tell you the truth?"

To her credit I ain't seen the red nor felt the juice these last couple seconds. But I also told the Almighty he could have my skills back. Maybe he took 'em just now, and I'm flyin' blind.

"Quick. What's your bra size?"

"Forty double D."

Got the juice, but just a touch.

"I'm bettin' thirty-eight."

She smile so tiny it couldn't give a flea wood. And the eyes narrow in like I arouse her suspicions, now 't she can't lie.

What a jolly world.

But I guess I still got the curse. At least the original. I don't care to test the snakes and skizzle.

"So, if I'm hearin' things right, you're a career girl."

"You're damn right."

"What was the better offer?"

"It was a perfect deal. In every way. They were going to give me a big story — the kind that gets picked up everywhere. And if I proved myself, you know, with the story, and whatever else they needed to get Wolfgang back ahead in the polls, then he'd win the election and we'd marry right after that. In January."

"Marry? Holy can a worms."

"What? It was a great deal."

"For a whore. You negotiate the job offer with it?"

"What, like with CNN? You never climbed the career ladder, apparently. You don't negotiate early when you're going to be in a more powerful position later. Sun Tzu said that, I think."

"I think it was Late Sue."

Flash a smile and cuss myself for breakin' the heavy mood, which was workin' in my favor. But she look at me dumb as a bowl of titted pudding, so nothin' lost.

Says I, "After the election y'all was gonna marry. You wrote up the story like he say, right?"

"Exactly. I didn't even write it, really. They gave me the story and I stylized it."

"So why they bring me in to kill you?"

"Excuse me?"

"Sure. Silas gimme your name, said you was next. I surmise he was part of Levi non-suicidin' himself. He run down Gretchen last night, by the underpass next the Hardgrave place. You was next on the kill list."

"And he sent you to do it."

"No one sends me anywhere. I ain't what you call an order taker."

"Soo.... You're on the FBI's most wanted list. I could scream your name right now — not saying I will — and everyone around us would know who you are."

"And you'd be dead."

"I understand that. I'm just asking... How does a murderer — no offense — who's running from the law connect with a politician who happens to be looking for a murderer to kill a reporter? That sounds like a question that could turn into a worthwhile story." She turn on me with chiselin' eyes. "How are you and Silas McClellan connected?"

I marvel a long second. She know who I am and what I'm capable of, and I already tell her enough most people'd be quakin' on the turd they just shat, but she's cool and steady, like her gaze alone give her the authority to demand the answer. And she sit on that hocum-pokum authority like the only outcome is me squirmin' 'til I confess a nugget.

But she ain't after the truth, only the commission she earn sellin' bullshit.

I let this woman go, she'll tell whatever lie makes the story. It's what she is, and things is rarely what they ain't.

"You're answerin' questions, not askin'. You already wrote the five hundred words. What was the meat?"

Just like when she agree to walk and then stand there lookin', now she sit still with nostrils wide and eyes steady.

Always the same with some types. You never get the honest self. Every word bounce off the barrier: what's in it for me and how'll I twist the situation to get advantage. Never the square conversation, words with information so I decide; you decide, we walk away content with our winnin's or losin's. What you get is words with in-built conclusions. People don't even know what an honest talk is.

These people.

I give her the opportunity.

Time for consequences.

Says I, "They's two outcomes. Come clean or die. More you ponder and scheme, the less utility you bring. No honest man'll have a use for ya. Whole world could benefit from rememberin' that."

"What use do I have with an honest man?"

She ain't takin' me serious. I lean. She lean. I look up the street a bit. No one facin' this way.

"Miss Preston, listen up."

She's real close.

I punch the flesh above her right knee, gouge the knuckles deep and twist. Her leg shoot out and she shriek. High heel fly twenty feet and land in the grass next a monument made outta spare car parts.

"Miss Preston, I get the sense you think we're on some kind of equal footin'. Think you got the wits to tangle me up and climb out the conversation in good shape. But I been killin' a lotta people, of late. I'm kinda dry to it, you know? Ain't impressed no more. It's tedious. Imagine killin' so many people it's tedious. That's who you're fuckin' with. Look at me."

She don't meet my eye.

I grab the back her head. We're in public but no one's close. I rotate her face to meet mine and lean in like we're lovers.

"So, you want your pretty hair to meet your pretty pillow tonight, and not a hole I dig on the Hardgrave land, some place back a the orchard, it's time to leave the games. Next time I need your attention I'll fire a bullet through your face to get it. You hear me?"

She hold the steady look two seconds 'til her brow wrinkles hard and the eyes fill with water.

"Go ahead and cry. I'll shoot your stupid ass right now."

She wipe her eye. Nod. Smile quick: you bust me, but I got great tits. Friends?

Every single move she make is corrupt. Says I:

"You need a three, two, one with a gun barrel at your head? What was the fuckin' meat?"

"Okay, okay... Levi... was ahead in the polls. Running for congress, incumbent had three terms... Levi was in the living room and saw where the fire started in the barn. He saw it in the back corner — that's the only part of the barn you can see from the sofa, through the window. The story had a couple quotes. Levi thought it was arson. It doesn't take much information to write a five-hundred-word story. That was it."

"Okay, so it was news. The barn burn."

"Right."

"Next story was the one they told you what to say."

"Uh-huh."

"What was in that? What Silas say to print?"

"The gist of it? Levi Hardgrave's campaign was out of money. Six weeks from the election and he's broke. So, he burned his barn to get the insurance claim."

"Don't make sense. What insurance company's gonna pay that fast?"

"He could use the insurance claim as collateral in a loan."

I'd say not, but greed and stupidity like holdin' hands. Lenders is pretty fuckin' greedy as a class, so who know?

"What proof he give?"

"What do you mean?"

"You shittin' me? Evidence."

"Uhm. I really don't want to antagonize you."

"Then tell the fuckin' truth. That's all you got to do."

"Proof — isn't how it works. We get stories. Packages, with characters and plots. We write narratives."

"With no evidence."

"Proof can be anything."

"Eye of the beholder, kinda thing."

"Exactly — or — someone else has seen the proof so we don't have to."

"Who's the someone?"

"Silas connected me with a forensic computer specialist in the NSA, and he said —"

"Whoa. Bullshit."

"What part?"

"The NSA? For a congress critter?"

She cock her head and that rack is lookin' marvelous agin.

"Fair 'nough. Where's this NSA feller? Dubois?"

"That's not how they work."

"Tell me."

"They contact you."

"And how you know who they are?"

"Reputation. History."

"You get stories off this feller afore?"

"No. But he promised —"

"You got a no-name witness. That's worse'n makin' it up."

Some color leave her face and she look a little better for it, frankly. Not so clowny with the makeup.

"No. I didn't make it up. But I'm afraid of you."

"That's the smartest thing you'll say this week. What this government man tell you?"

"Well, it was all for national security. With the country being infiltrated by terrorists and everything, he said he had no choice but to go public with the information. Better to have me expose Levi Hardgrave before the election, than have him win and be susceptible to blackmail."

"By Arabs with boxcutters. Sure. Accourse. What information?"

"Levi did a bunch of computer searches looking for accelerants."

"You mean like to start a fire."

"Yes."

"Ok. How he know?"

"What do you mean?"

"Either the NSA has a man or woman watchin' every single person in the country while they do their business on the internet, or they got a record, and this fella decide to look in on one congress critter, see what he could find."

"I don't know how he knew."

"And you never work with this man afore?"

Head shake.

"You meet him? Or talk on the phone?"

"The phone."

"So, you talk to somebody who said some shit, is all. Who you get to back it up?"

"Yes. Of course. As a rule, we don't print stories without corroboration. But when the source is a highly placed NSA official familiar with the matter —"

"Who you don't know, never see and talk to once..."

Eyebrow shrug. "It was a matter of national security. That's why I couldn't meet the man. He was putting himself out on a limb, going against the government and everything."

"I'm gettin' dizzy. You bring stupidity to a new height. How's fakin' dirt on the challenger goin' agin' the government?"

"What do you expect? Him to say he's a super secret spy agent, but he'll expose his identity for the truth?"

"Yeah. Sure, that'd be good. You know words. What're they worth without a reputation behind 'em?"

She seem exasperated by her lack of knowledge and slow intelligence.

"Even better," says I, "once you get the man's ass on the record, then find another source or six, since your story was bound to change the election."

Now she look like I'm the idiot.

"Weren't you listening? That was the whole point. To change the election. Wolfgang was losing and we needed to —"

Put my hand up.

"I heard enough."

I stand.

"What are you doing?"

She shrink to the bench. "You said you were giving me a chance to make it right."

"I did."

CHAPTER TWENTY-SEVEN

I step off from the bench pretty damn sure ol' Heidi's due for the dirt. But time I'm fifty yards off, my mind been through the mill.

Look back and she got her cell phone in the air, aimed my way.

How these people work with the technology, I mighta just fuck myself. But since I ain't pretendin' to do the Lord's work I sense relief tyin' these last strings. Two more in a bow and I'm outta here, and vow not to get tangled in any new evil 'til I find Tat and my baby.

I don't know if I'm makin' the world any better. Killin' liars is like pullin' dandelions. Two more take the space.

It's almost like killin' ain't the answer.

But a world chock fulla treachery, with near every word said an outright lie or a tricky sales pitch, so a neighbor can't trust a neighbor let alone the law, that world'll fall of its own corrupt weight anyhow. Anyone fightin' agin it's on the side of good, somewhere, and if it ain't official good then fuck the official. It's time to find a new official. A new morality. The old ain't carryin' water.

Right? Or not?

Under one man or another's heartfelt logic, we all need put down. It's a good thing most men and women don't got the stones to cross the line, but if I think back on the lives I took and whether I'm sure the world's a better place without 'em, they's no contest. As a rule, I only kill folk in profound need of killin'.

Wanderin' thought. Like red herring.

The Almighty can kill easier'n me. Better'n me.

And he done a hell of a lot more of it.

Can a just killin' be unholy? Is all killin' unholy? Or is all my murder right and good if it was done by God, and evil if it was done by me?

How can that be? Things is what they is. Ain't what they ain't. If it's good that the men I sent forward is forward, then it don't matter to the good whether I put 'em down, or God, or some useless mess o' bureaucrats think they run shit. The end's the end. If the end is good, why ain't the means — 'less the goal ain't reachin' the end but preservin' the means.

Cartels everywhere. Guilds. Mafiosos and thugs. All power's abused; the more power the more abuse. A is A. *It is what it is. Seldom what it ain't*, said Aristotle.

'Specially the ones in robes. But fuck all that. Justice is justice and a just man don't need twelve others to know he's just. He only has to be willin' to bear the consequence when the corrupt protect their turf.

We liars and thieves on top the social order — justice is our domain. And the fuckers don't know justice, never seen it and won't 'til it splits their brains, like Silas was introduced a little while back.

Fuck all that. I wouldn't give a mangy rat's left nut for any man's opinion, as I know the general quality of his thinkin' and the deceit wove into his soul. Ponderin' man is naught but noise. Fuck man.

I was tryin' to think on the Almighty, but I ain't so fruitful as others.

Almighty's hard to pin down; men, not so hard.

So, this last bit of business ahead is for me. Maybe lance the fury, let the pus drain so I can get busy pullin' the timber out my eye. Live more good. Whatever the hell that'll entail.

Only killin' when I really, really think I oughtta.

Free thinkin' ain't easy, but failin' is slavery, body and soul. I won't even be a slave to the one who made me, and I got to believe that's the way he wants it. Otherwise, why give me both a mind and a spine? I'll respect him and fear him, but I won't be a slave.

Stance like that don't leave much room to tolerate evil men, neither. So, I'm back where I was on day one.

The roads is comin' easier, now I seen the main thoroughfares a couple time. I head back for the poisoned land of Walnut, Pennsylvania while ideas slow cook in the noggin. Park at the camp. Empty the bladder on a rock so I can watch my piss splash 'til I see how much is gettin' on my boots, then arc to the crick and find the splash there equally satisfyin'.

Drained, I see where I left the last jug o' walnut shine. I'm moved to chuck it while I got the cold logic and feel less susceptible. But I get it in the hand and the indecision cut through me, and I set it back down.

Maybe I'll need a dose 'fore fightin' the spectre. Maybe it'll take a couple good snurgles just to see him.

But the Almighty gimme the impulse: I grab the neck, follow through with a couple steps of windup and hurl that glass jug to the closest hemlock and watch as it cross the crick, end over end, black poison splashin' inside...

... and bounce off the wood, land soft in the dirt, upright, like a stone in the shoe I'll step on long as I'm near these parts.

Temptation, ever present.

Sometimes it feels like the Almighty give us weakness for sport. Book of Job, and all.

So I pull Smith and shoot the jug.

I'm done with it.

I cut to the woods for where I saw the porcupine and there turn right and follow the bottom grade of the highway 'til I reach the road that cut up from the woods where they run down Gretchen in the night.

I said to Heidi it was Silas, run her over and back up to do it agin, but I can't say if it was someone else. And that make me wonder on the last fella these devil worshippers took in. Who'd they use to whack Levi Hardgrave? What become of him, that they need me to stop in this ornery pocket of hell?

Where's the last killer buried, is the question, and who put the bullet in his head?

Did he talk to the Almighty too?

The wife knew and was part, but she couldn't make ice tea let alone murder a man.

Silas coulda run down Gretchen. Fact — the way she died'd

be the most convenient way to kill, for an old fat man likes lady bugs on his cushions.

Even not knowin' how he done it, I'm glad Silas is dead. What he did to Carpenter the Yank Dog easily merits the bullet. If I'd known for sure he did Gretchen I mighta cut off his nuts too. I dunno.

Comin' up on the road I get high on the embankment, up next the concrete bridge, lookin' down.

Terrain gimme a good vantage. Gretchen's still there, hostin' three turkey buzzards, the ugliest condor-lookin' creatures ever built. Livin' gargoyles.

"Hiya!"

Nothin'.

"Get the fuck outta here!"

Pull Smith and shit.

Car comin' through the underpass from the McClellan side. Prius swerve and stop.

Heidi Preston pop out the car and aim her phone at the body. Got no situational awareness. She's talkin' all along, so I guess maybe it's video. Any luck, she's broadcastin' live to the world.

"Heidi," says I, leavin' my perch by the concrete and steppin' down the slope.

She point the phone at me.

"It's him. He's here," says she.

"Howdy," says I. "Who you got on the other end?"

"The Associated Press."

"Good."

I swing Smith. Point, but don't quite aim.

"The entire world is watching you aim that gun at me. You'll never get away with it."

Red. Juice. Snakes.

"I guess I promised the ballyhoo, so here goes. In a minute I'm gonna send you forward. Don't worry, as the bullet'll turn your entire head to mist faster'n you can feel it. The worst part of your dyin's right now, while you still think you might find a way to squirm out your fate. You can't though, as it's your own fruit bearin' down.

"Relax while I walk you through this. Once that bullet turn your brain to chunky soup, all that juice that was your thinkin' — well that's electricty, see. Einstein said they's naught but energy. Mags too. It don't disappear. So that juice'll stay, and your spiritual self'll mosey off, a little outta sorts without a body. You remember that episode of MASH, way back? Walkin' down the road with the other dead people? This you ain't the real you, is what I'm sayin'. Good thing, 'cause this you sucks, and you wouldn't want to be a bitch for eternity, right? Kinda defeat the purpose of all these lessons you're 'bout to pay for.

"I'm gettin' off track. Anyway, while your body's yet wettin' your undies one final time, you'll be off with your Maker. This is known by science. He'll help you see how fuckin' foul you been, and you'll suffer so much that even the most vengeful, hatin'est sonufabitch like me'll feel satisfied you found a fair reward.

"Then you party. You're back with the good. This whole poisoned fuckin' existence of yours on earth'll be wisdom in your eternal soul, so next time, in the Kingdom, you won't carry on the way you did in this one. So selfish and all. Make sense?"

"That's the ballyhoo?"

Smile.

"You're stark raving mad."

"That's excessive. I — well, I do confess I believe the world is nuts, so it's me or y'all. Either way I got the gun."

She got a point but not what she think. I see it all exposed bare. Understandin' so clean it has to be holy:

That's why the liars do it. So many untruths pile up from the first words out Momma's mouth. You a good little baby. White lies, black lies, things people know but can't say. Truth ain't natural; never was.

It took the curse to wake me to it as a boy.

Heidi say, "I'm taking video and broadcasting to the internet right now."

"No, you ain't. Happy travels."

Ten feet off I get serious on my aim, figurin' one to the forehead'll suffice.

"Wait!"

"Huh?"

"Why? What did I do?"

"Well funny you should ask. I forgot that part. Once you're in the nonlocal, you'll relive each moment. Your whole life to this point here at the end. You'll see yourself through other people's eyes and know their thoughts. You ain't seen truth your whole life. I'm sure you can wait another few —"

Fire Smith and her head snaps hard. She fall back and the legs don't move. Arms don't flap. Nothin'. Just a dead woman's body hittin' dirt.

Tinny voice:

"Hey! Hey! Who are you? Pick up the phone."

Sure.

Cell phone in her hand. I grab it and see naught but a

number pad and red button. If Heidi was shootin' video it don't work like Tat's phone.

This one-time, Tat took film of me in a brook naked, scrubbin' my nethers. Colder'n shit. Dick like a grub worm. She laugh and laugh.

"You motherfucker! Pick up the phone!"

"Hold your horses. Say your name."

"Who are you? Murderer!"

"Okay. Well, you got my name, what's yours?"

"I'm coming for you," the voice say.

"For who? Heidi?"

"For you."

"Good."

Now I got fingerprints on the phone I best keep it. Cross the road while I shovel Smith back to my hip. No cars. Wonder why they made a road. I head back the way I come.

"Tell me, mister. You know where to find me?"

"Exactly."

"I doubt, but I'll take your word. You the NSA feller, by any chance?"

Snicker. Huff. "Is she dead? Did you kill her?"

"You'll find her by the bridge. It was quicker'n she deserve. Don't expect the same favor."

I press the red button. Walkin' the woods back to the truck I slip off the battery cover and drop the juice pack under a rock next the stream. Then think on that acid or whatever, and the fish, and retrieve the battery. Up by the porcupine tree I find another with rotted innards and drop it inside.

Phone's got my prints. I grab a fist of mud and scrub my hands and the cell. Listen. No cars above on the highway just now, so I chuck the cell high and wait to hear it bust on cement and take the lack of sound as evidence it cleared the first two lanes. Good enough.

Take my time enjoyin' the crick, the moss so thick I could use it for a pillow, pools here and there with tiny crawfish and minnows. A whole different world with sunlight in it.

At camp I sit in the International and ponder how I'm gonna deal with the devil.

CHAPTER TWENTY-EIGHT

ALL THE POISON I DRUNK THESE LAST COUPLE DAYS — OR thirty years — has my innards in a mess and my spirit low. I stretch with knees folded and my back and stockinged feet on the seat. Got my boots airin' in the footwell and the windows open to help relieve the odoriferousness. Naturally the skeeters is out and the sun keep findin' a direct path through the leaves and hemlock to keep a bolt in one dozin' eye or the other, as the late afternoon unwinds to evenin'. At last, the sun's near disappeared and the skeeters that carried off three buckets of blood musta told all the rest in the woods, and they come huntin' too.

I never fed Smith after he done his day's work. And since the fella on the phone said he was comin' for me, and my dozin' body's got almost no blood left to offer the skeeters, I swing my legs down and sit. About time I go up and find the sonofabitch, assumin' it was indeed the congressman from Walnut.

Reachin' under the seat for a box of shells I come up empty — I never move 'em from the Eldorado.

I got but one bullet left.

Wouldn't call it a pickle, yet. Back in the day I hear the krauts lined up prisoners to see how many they could kill with one bullet goin' through all 'em. Wish they tested the ol' Smith & Wesson Model 29. Gotta be a couple fellas, easy. Trick is usin' the right words to get 'em in a line.

Regardless I got one shot. It ain't a pickle necessarily; just that sometimes I like to shoot a fella more'n once.

I check my pocket, find another shell, feed Smith his ration.

We all got to tighten our belts from time to time. At this juncture I could eat squirrel guts.

Belly's like a woman won't shut up.

Lord I miss Tat.

That headache from afore I sent the McClellans forward disappear sometime after. Now with a decent nap I don't feel head pain so much as lazy pain. If I could put the windows up and sleep all night I would. All the woods is gray with dusk.

Sometimes it take a minute after a decision to get the gumption to follow through — 'specially if the decision involves physical movement. I sit in the truck and let my breath gather, and my mind percolate some awakeness through it, and hope a happy thought'll catch me.

But it's dusk.

Good thing I shot that jug.

Wonder if any shine maybe sits in a curved shard or two. A sip?

Or if any jugs is left in the Hardgrave house?

If I got to take on that demon locus satan whateverthefuck

fallen angel — which sound about as horse shit a story I ever hear; what angel's dumb 'nough he mistake himself for his Maker — more like he was made broke from the getgo like the rest of us — well if I got to do battle with pure evil, and can't see 'im 'less I'm snookered on walnut shine, it's meet and good if I imbibe the spirit so I can kill a spirit.

'Cause they ain't no way in hell I'll figger how to do it sober.

Open the truck door.

Another five second pass and I got the ambition to move my left leg out. A good deep breath and I don't feel better but move the left leg to follow. Slip out, grab the door, wait on the legs to rouse full strength, and once the blood start pumpin' and the woozy leave my head, I find the skillet with the bacon grease still in it, drag a finger 'tween the flies and drop a curd of mushy salty fat to the tongue.

People don't eat pork — now I understand people got choices —

Crash!

Windshield pop in a giant spider web with the middle blasted out on the hood, and the instant I think they musta put new glass in, as the shatter proof stuff ain't original, I also figger the bullet musta pass through the open driver side where the window woulda been if I didn't put it down. Otherwise, what part of the windshield that blew out woulda landed on the seat.

I got a shitty shooter in front, maybe fifty yards out to miss a target so easy. Usin' a pistol. And I bet from the clap it's a nine, a .38, whatever.

Enough to hurt.

Then I understand I got the pre-thinkin' goin' on, seein'

moments unfold slow, or me thinkin' fast, and all at once as I throw my lookin' outward, I don't see 'em so much as know 'em.

They's three men out there, shadows ain't right, forms a-closin' in. I figger 'em in a single glance.

And if they send three from the front they's at least one comin' from behind they want to drive me to, if they can't kill me outright.

And I got two bullets.

Let's get it the fuck on.

CHAPTER TWENTY-NINE

Attackin' backward ain't retreat when you got two bullets.

My best thinkin's to take out the one comin' from behind as that'll afford a new weapon and what distance I can gain. Problem is these fellas up front is keepin' a steady fusillade, and to be honest if I didn't half wish to send my self forward and see what all the hubbub's about, this situation'd skew toward terrifyin'.

I hunker and a bullet pop through the door next my head. Another to the bed on my left. I had a sense where they was at first and now it's just bullets punchin' the International.

Maybe I get a little lower...

Engine's thicker'n truck bed so I crawl thataway.

Can't believe these fellers is such bad aims. Man gotta stand up and point at his chest?

And that gimme the gumption, as if I truly wanted dead

they's easy ways to make it happen, and don't rely on piss poor marksmen to get 'er done.

I got enough bullets for that job, if the job was wantin' done.

I push off and lift up, and the next incomin' crease my arm like a hornet sting.

Git low agin. Them bullets is like I bust a nest of 'em.

Guns fire from all three angles in front and side to side. I try and think how many, but without knowin' the number each man start with I'm wastin' time.

If I can't find a path 'round the truck —

I look out and see the first of 'em, man in a deep blue jacket. I bet he got some letters on the back. Make sense — what modern leader you know fight his own fight? A snake like to use Heidi to ruin a man, he ain't gonna throw a punch in the open. He'll send another while he sneak up behind.

Regardless, this lawman in the jacket ain't but twenty feet out and if he was sharper with the eyeballs, he'd see me through the rough.

Lord, I thank you for all the little plants.

Roll on my back, git half in under the truck and pull my head up 'nough to see past my feet. I can spot the movement but not the man. Hard to focus the eyeballs with the head strain — but he ain't too far off neither — and got a cleaner line o' sight.

So, this is it.

I know these so-called lawmen don't know the final rites, and the congressman don't strike me as like to be enlightened. While I ponder the way out, I got to entertain the notion I met my end.

Maybe it's time.

I drop back my head and look up into the closin' dark. Hemlock limbs is out and though they could be jagged and mean, I get more of a homey comfort from 'em, as I spent so many evenin' in North Carolina with Fred and the others — Loretta was a fine puppygirl — I like to think on her from time to time. I spent so many nights lookin' through the limbs and ponderin' the Almighty up there, it's a mild comfort to see the same view.

On my back, starin' up into the big empty, I give myself the full ballyhoo:

I, Baer Creighton, been a mean piece of work.

I was nasty when I didn't need to be.

Selfish and ornery.

I never stole, only when it was necessary. But I'm so fuckin' proud I use it to hang my neighbor. Shoot him. Poison him. Whatever else ways I killed. Mostly shootin'.

I like the titties too much.

I wasn't a father. I hid. Still hide.

I was never the bigger man, always the smaller. Always quick to come back mean and dirty. Never first to let a trespass go.

I can't remember forgivin' no one nothin', 'less I didn't care to begin with.

I see my neighbor's lies but never his truth.

I see the liar as the enemy, not my brother to save from the dark.

Hell, I don't even see my own dark.

I think on titties an awful lot, is the truth.

I quit tryin' to do good, on the license I'm saved by the Lord, anyway.

I get carried away with the foul words.

Can't be healthy, much as I think on titties.

I'm sure they's a hundred more but time's short.

I bring my Maker shame, and I don't want to die so much as disappear.

When the bullets fill me with holes and my soul slips out through 'em, I'll've earned as much sufferin' as I get. More.

I'll pass through the white tunnel and see the forms on the other side. The nonlocal side, which Mags say is everywhere and nowhere. All connected. Deep and thick. Untouchable and unknowable, 'til I'm in it, of it, am it.

Livin' where thoughts is terrain and holiness flows through like streams and rivers.

When I get there, I'll crumble afore my Maker deservin' no pity at all. None, as I heard Him whisper a million times I was off the mark and didn't change my ways. I'll get on my knees, but I won't beg His mercy as I earned whatever wrath I got comin'.

Then He'll show me each of my life's moments agin, through the eyes of the men and women I hurt, so I feel the words I shot at others puncture my own heart and make me weak. I'll recoil from my own fury when I'm its target. I'll wish I was never born, for the sake of all the people's paths I darkened.

And when I seen my entire life beginnin' to end, I'll see why it all makes sense. Why both the Almighty's books says I'm the problem.

In my heart I invent the evil. Its what I learn and so its what I choose. I see it where it is, and I make it where it ain't.

I never let the Almighty renew my mind, so to let me invent the love instead.

It's like Mags say. The only true path is love.

And when the Lord's done teachin' and I'm a puddle of self hate and tears, he'll gather me close, redeemed and newly tolerable, and send me off to see my mother.

And the brother I failed to keep.

CHAPTER THIRTY

The bullets stop a long second while I'm deliverin' myself over, just as I commend the Lord to take me if it's His will or leave me if it ain't.

Open the eyes and the sky's the same — like a bare half minute transpire.

Reloadin'?

All 'em?

Zap! Splash!

Pistol bang!

What the sam — that come from the middle but back some.

Zap! Splash!

Pistol bang!

Tat? She nail two men that fast?

The fuck?

Sound's familiar for sure, Tat's Sig. She fire it so many times this summer it's like hearin' her voice all soft and lovey.

I roll and pop on my knees. Skitter 'round the front bumper low's I can, and this big feller's half hid behind a — can't tell if it's maple or beech, with the bark fairly smooth and the dusk closin' in. I bet it's maple, is how I lean. But this feller's got his knee out and I —

Zap! Bang!

No splash. C'mon Tat. Get your shit together.

Zap! Bang!

Tat?

I lay flat with both hands on the grip and while I gather a good aim on the legislator's knee, I spot his pistol above, a sliver of black exposed. He's twenty feet off if that. I can shoot a gnat that far, or wing 'im.

"Hey feller. Congressman, that you?"

The tree says nothin'.

"I see your gun. And your knee. Bit o' your ass." He move but can't get all himself behint cover. "I can put a bullet through any 'em I want, but I ain't, on account I kill too many men already. See ordinarily I'd just put you down, as you're lowlife. Hell, you know that. But I got inspired a minute ago and, well — you want to give yourself up and not die, and confess your sins to the world on camera, so we can —"

He push his gun out quick and fire nowhere.

Boom!

No zing? Not even close. From the silhouette and sound, I'm sayin' a 1911, .45ACP. But any make and caliber'd give sufficient indication the prick don't want justice. He want dominion. He want his ways over mine, and he come out here with his boys to do as he saw fit as the bigger meaner man.

Me goin' outside the rules to enforce 'em ain't the same as him goin' outside the rules to break 'em, and —

Zing-Boom!
Gett'in' closer.
Okay — the way it is.

Hands folded on Smith and restin' on dirt, I line them sights in the dimmin' light on part of the gun hand he left exposed, then shift my aim close the tree so if I miss, it's to the right and maybe I chip 'm with maple. Slow and patient I let the air out my lungs, wait on empty and squeeze...

Smith barks a boom and it's all motion behint the tree.

Boom! Zing!

"Argg! Fuck!"

Hand flyin' out and pullin' back. Pistol float in the air. Knee way out. Got him disarmed and bloody.

Fuck it, I aim for the knee.

Zap! Splash!

Pistol Bang!

Good girl, Tat! Good girl! That's the last bad guy of the three that come from the front.

Fella by the tree — now his knee's hid.

And his ass is hangin' out the other side. I pull the trigger.

Boom! Thunk!

"Argg Fuuuuaaaahck!"

"Shoulda picked a tree with a bigger ass 'n you!" says I.

He's outta fucks and I'm outta bullets. I send Smith home to holster and squiggle forward, get to knees, launch best I can off my bad leg as I ain't thinkin' clear for all the excitement. He's fallin' back and floppin' over — and shit if his hand ain't a quinny hair from the pistol I chip out his hand.

If I put a forty four magnum through his Glock, I bet the Glock's dead. But if I chipped the tree and wood peeled the

Glock out that man's hand, the pistol'll be ready to shoot soon as it's back in his hand.

I swoop down and it's like the Almighty put the river rock in my hand. Legs got the wobble. I miss a step and stumble. Swing my arm up 'round the head and over like a Old Book stonin'.

I watch that sandstone fly and the congressman watch it fly so fast he don't move 'til it bust his face.

His hand quit its quest. I get there quick and grab the Glock.

"Brother," says I. "You got any mind to know what's next?"

Zap! Splash!

Half his head's popped open. Ain't much gray inside.

"Fuckin' A, Tat. I was talkin' to this man!"

I turn.

Don't see nobody.

"Tat?"

Step back. Look 'bout for cover, 'cept I don't know what from. I know Tat's gun, I think. Pretty sure I know Tat's gun.

"Tat?"

She's skinny 'nough to hide behind a blade a grass — if it had pert little — see there I go agin. There I go.

Irredeemable.

Incorrigible.

I need to focus on my corrige, and not the titties so much.

As I been redeemed, I see the path the Almighty gimme to walk. He made it clear. I never see anything so clear as my own broke soul.

I can't walk that way no more. I can't walk that trail.

I drop the Glock. Pull out Smith and drop him too. You serve me well, mighty Smith, but it's quits.

I'm done. Changin' my ways from here on out.

"Tat? Dear Sweetie Love, whatever I said afore when I was out my mind on the walnut shine, I ain't out my mind no more. I'm walkin' a crystal path through fields 'o love. A changed man. Inspired to do my utmost. I'll be clean and sober, here on out. Chock fulla love and tenderness. The Almighty spare me — with you as His righteous instrument. C'mon up here and give ol' Baer a kiss. Holy Lord! I'm alive! Woop!"

Ah, shit. Here come the wet eyes.

I get to see my boy!

Twig crack and I spot a pistol barrel ease out from behint another tree. Close to dark and my eyesight's filmy, I'm guessin' it's hemlock from the scrubby bare limbs above. A skinny arm follow the pistol and half a beautiful head. And just like that the handgun find its focus, dead on my heart.

Tat step out.

I put the hands up. Water come from the eyes and it's all I can do to see her through the wash. I blink but my lids don't clear the wet. Shake my head. Fall to knees, spread the arms and bring 'em low, from the feelin' of holy sorrow I carry for these dead men and my soul-wounded woman.

I know the Almighty didn't save the old Baer Creighton.

The Almighty made him new, and it hurt.

CHAPTER THIRTY-ONE

MAN DON'T GOTTA DESERVE A GOOD WOMAN TO WANT ONE. Accourse when the one he choose put a pistol on him he don't want her good so much as forgivin', and the two ain't always the same.

"Why did you do that?" says she.

"What?"

Tat lower the Sig and point at Smith.

"I'm done addin' to the world's misery."

Tat shake her head. I'm wrong.

"I'm done thinkin' killin' is the first and best option?"

She still shakin' her noggin', and add a half-frown plus a head tilt. Gettin' warmer... I think...

"The gun's heavy in the hand? I'll think on it later?"

Now she just blank.

"Shit, Tat. I didn't want this life. Never did. I grew up quiet, got the curse and just want to be left alone. But people get in my shit. People fuck with me, not the other way 'round.

I give people the straight truth. I deal square. All I ask in return. But some folk view an honest man as a mark, and I can't sit for that. I never went lookin' for it, but I sure as fuck can't sit for some lyin' sack a —"

See there Almighty? See? I can't help but rise up. I'm proud. On account I ain't a lyin' piece a shit. Can't a man at least be proud he ain't a fuckin' liar? A cheat? A politician?

I nudge the dead congressman like I'm ten-year-old kickin' air.

Look at Tat and she ain't been privy to most of what I figure out that matters.

"Why did you stop speaking and kick him?"

"Feel like I chewed my own ass and fart in my mouth."

"Brush your teeth."

"Worth a kiss if I do?"

Tat still got her head a little off kilter and with the dusky light and the way I'm deeper in the cover and she's more toward the clearin', there, her figure's dark with the light behind, and I'm overwhelmed with so much sinful thinkin' I can't stay on the straight and narrow.

"A poke, maybe?"

I'm fast-thinkin' agin, and grok a minute on how bein' next a woman like Tat can't help but lead a man to carnal thinkin', and it's my own misguided righteousness 'bout feelin' guilty as a fifty-three-year-old man screwin' a eighteen year old girl and fuckin' lovin' it, that I never drop a knee and ask her to make it right afore God and man.

"I don't know," says she. "What if I need protection. I need a real man."

"I'm a real man."

Shrug and tilt. Smile. "Maybe. I don't know."

"Maybe, shit." Jostle my mess. "You know what I'm packin'."

"You aren't going to defend me with that."

The Almighty's testin' me. Or is he? Tat want me to pick up Smith and go on the way we was goin', killin' in every town we land in. But I got to turn from that life.

I don't want to die, but this ain't 'bout mortal life and death. It's eternal. I'm at war with my own soul and always been. But I don't want war I want peace. And if I gotta be near people, honest people, I want quiet. A good dog and a good woman. I want the biological stuff. I keep killin' right and left, this way and that, I won't have any of the good peaceable me left. Or a soul, so much as a shadow.

In my core I know I got to do my utmost to preserve a life, and not be so eager to take it. I got to trust more in the miracle and less in Smith. But the miracle not comin' forthwith, post hence, A-the-fuck SAP, I got to handle business. He gimme a mind and gun both.

I got it figured, yessir.

I'm guessin' this is the moment, so I drop my right knee, smile back the wince on account Tat's eyes just pop out her head and I don't want me lookin' funny when she remember the moment, as women is prone. I grab Smith and shovel him home, grab Tat's pistol hand and with the Sig pointed at my heart and her careless finger in the trigger housin':

"Tat, I love you. I'll always love you and I'll defend you with my no-reserve best if you'll marry me right now in the eyes of the Almighty."

Her hand move under mine and I confess a spark in my brain touch off a small fire; is she pullin' the trigger?

"Let go."

I let her hand go.

Tat say: "If I would have jerked away — your hand — I would have pulled the trigger."

That's fear in her look. Raw.

She punch me, girl-wise, and I know she know how to throw a real punch, so I take it as the signal and yank her back to me. Close the arms on her with the Sig between us pointed left or right one, but not in either our guts.

Tat say, "Name one person you killed that you would allow to date our daughter."

"None. Not a one."

Tat roll her eyes. They's pretty in the growin' dark.

"What? You sayin' — What? A girl! How you know?"

"I went to the doctor. They did a test."

"How far... along...?"

"Four months."

"What?"

"Baer! Which of the men that we killed would you trust alone with your daughter?"

"None."

"Aren't we trying to make a world where we can trust all of them?"

CHAPTER THIRTY-TWO

"Sounds good and all. Mighty good. But I can't be killin'. Not as the first and best option. It ain't. I'm addin' to the world's misery, not subtractin'."

"Until the man you refuse to deal with molests another girl. Then you are adding."

"Refuse to deal with? I'm dealin' everywhere. Every sin. Like I'm the Lord's hall monitor, but carryin' a Smith & Wesson."

"You said he appointed you."

"Well, shit. Now I'm judged for both what I do and don't do."

"Only a coward finds virtue in hiding."

"A coward! Society got police for law and order."

She gimme a puckered mouth.

"Okay," says I. "Good point."

"My father was a policeman. A chief. But it is the same here as where I came from. The police do not exist so everyone else can be a coward."

Call me a coward twice. Unsettlin' words.

"I didn't propose an argument, so much as a quick weddin' here in the woods, while they's yet a little light."

"I cannot marry a fool."

When I put Tat's Sig at my chest, I thought the gun was the most likely way she'd break my heart.

Not so.

I drop the arms. Step back. Let her words punch and kick while I gather myself a long second or five.

"We live in a wicked world," Tat say. "I will not raise a child with a man who believes his words are stronger than his bullets."

It ain't that.

"It ain't that. I got to let the Almighty do some the savin', is all. My soul ain't big 'nough to write the law. Nor force my will all over the place, like I'm the source of all that's good and light and true. I'm a blind man walkin' 'round with a bunch of other blind men, killin' 'em. They done evil. I done evil."

She look at me and I look at her. I ain't yet said it but I find the kernel and voice it:

"If I'm redeemable, why ain't they?"

Chipmunk or somethin' rustle some leaves.

"I ain't right with the Almighty. I can feel it."

Tat look past me a while and her eyes is wet.

"Your Almighty had the opportunity to save Corazon, twice."

"That ain't —"

"Twice! The first time he failed, and you saved me and then

I saved her. The second time God, you, me, none of us were there for her. I don't trust three times."

I'm doin' math: technically I only fail her once, and that on account she don't drive a car for shit. But some truth ain't worth airin'.

Twig snap off'n my right, behin' Tat.

She freeze, her stare on my eyes and I turn mine.

"Drop it!"

Sizable man in a suit and tie.

"Ah shit. Here we fuckin' go."

They was five men, not four. This one leadin' from behind. I give Tat the narrow look, says don't try nothin'.

"I didn't think that feller I popped with the stone look a congress critter. But you do. Fuckin' suit and tie in the woods."

"Drop the pistol, woman."

Tat's face is mad and mean and since she's eyeballin' me, and he's behind her, I expect I'm the source and destination. Inside it's like I let my mother down, or God if he was a woman. I'm alone fieldin' all Tat's fear and hate and it's witherin'.

"He got us, Tat. Better drop the pistol," says I.

Can't wink nor give a signal.

"Time to trust the Lord's mysterious ways," says I. "Love, put the pistol down. This feller got us in a bind."

She glare. Snarl.

"Drop it, lady," says the congressman. "I won't say it again."

Tat bend slow, reach a bit, and rest the Sig on a half-rotted log.

"All right. We good a minute. Like I say, mister congress. I got a question."

"Pick up that man's radio," says Wolfgang McClellan.

"Sure. But I gotta give fair warnin'. I'm fairly tight with the Almighty, I gather from recent events. Odds is pretty good he'll be callin' you home soon."

"You killed Press," says he.

"Heidi, you mean, and *sent her forward* is the parlance. By now most likely she's through the hurtful part and I bet she's already mended her ways. She's in good shape."

"She said you were crazy. Now move slowly and take the radio off that man's belt."

"I will. But I ain't crazy, just sighted, is all. Less inspired by the mortal world and more the one beyond. I know you're itchin' to shoot, but I gotta ask a question — and this is more for the benefit of the woman here."

"The only question on my mind is why I haven't shot you both yet."

"That's the exact same question I got. But I know the answer and you don't."

"Is that so?"

"It is."

"Are you going to tell me?"

"I want you to know."

He lift his chin like a tough guy actin' tougher.

"The Almighty put a hex on you. Fact is, it's lucky you found us at all. Most times when the Almighty put on the hex, it's like fishin' for bass. You ever fish?"

He shake his head.

All I'm doin' is keepin' him confused', buyin' time. From Tat's eyes, she think I'm waitin' on a thunderbolt from heaven.

I ain't.

"You never go bass fishin'? When I was a boy, see, we had this fishin' hole. Me and my brother Larry'd go there, and we grew up poor, right? One time I had to make my own hooks outta coat hanger and a file. Bein' poor we didn't have proper swim attire, neither. You understand? We'd fish with a stick and line, and we'd swim in the natural. The buff. The bare ass naked."

"Why did you kill Press?"

"Hold on a minute; this is important for your understandin'. You ever hear a dick fishin'?"

McClellan jab the air with his gun. "We're done." He aim his pistol dead on my face so it's lookin' mighty narrow. Dead on.

"Oh yeah, dick fishin's a thing — but only with the bigger guys, if you follow. But you never hear of it? I wonder why."

If this is the moment I get to head forward myself, and this is what the Almighty want, then I'm skippy with it.

But Stinky Joe ain't.

He been creepin' like a cat these last couple minute, and six feet back, fast as an eye can blink, Stinky Joe hurl himself from the ground to McClellan's back.

I jump sideways and push Tat too.

Joe climb the big man with a single bound and plant his jaws on back his neck. Wolfgang lurch and Joe ride 'im to his knees. Tat dive for the Sig but time she got it in hand, Joe's ripped off half the congressman's neck, lassoed him with teeth and split the big vein.

Stinky Joe's weight flop him too far and Wolfgang swing a half dead arm, pistol in hand, and Tat fire lead through his gun shoulder.

Tat's on the ground and Joe's launchin' agin, but that pistol's still a viable killer so I jump thataway and see the flash, hear the whistle-zip then the bang, and if that ain't confirmation I'm supposed to raise a girl named Moxie, I don't know what is.

I pass from McClellan's aim, and he can't get back on me as Joe's got his arm and I put a boot in his face, then drop both knees on his pistol arm while Stinky Joe go to work on the other half his neck.

McClellan don't resist but a second more. Wheezin' blood. Chokin', now.

I look off while the snarlin' and gurglin's goin' on, as I no longer go the constitution.

Let the eye meet Tat and mouth *I love you*.

She gimme a batshit look, shift her gaze to Wolfgang, then Joe, still gnawin' neck, then back at me transformed.

Gimme a schoolgirl simper.

Wolfgang got a husky moan in his bloody gurgle and quit movin' altogether.

While I got it in mind, I pull the Glock out his hand, unpin his arm and chuck the pistol in the crick.

He's dead a long minute afore Tat say, "That wasn't a miracle. It was Joe."

"Yeah. Well, Joe's a fuckin' miracle."

CHAPTER THIRTY-THREE

"We still have something to talk about," says Tat.

"Shush" I get on both my knees. "C'mere Joe. Tat, c'mon now."

Spread the arms like — I'm charged as a fool; first word come to mind is a eagle.

Spread my arms all eagle-like and gather mine to me. Scruffin' Joe's back and Tat's too. We close 'round Joe and love on each other a minute, celebratin' kinship and warmth. A couple too many skeeters want in, and after I sneak my lips next Tat's neck, get the nose back in her hair and sweaty neck, it's all I can do to not say any word I got to say to win her.

But I'm set.

"Stinky Joe, shit. Joe, I love ya. Tat, I love ya."

I stand and put Smith in Tat's hand, stoop to Joe one more time and cup his cheek. "You and me been through some shit, ain't we?"

We've faced challenges. And we've always been there.

Joe's eyes is knit and he ain't quite comprehendin' the dynamic.

"What is this?" Tat say. "What are you doing?"

"I got one fight left, and it's mine alone and that gun won't do any good anyhow."

"I am coming."

"You'll not."

I keep her gaze and somethin' three thousand feet back in my heart come up through my look and she understand she better do as I say, as sometimes a man'll know what's better best.

Back a step, another.

"Hey!" says I, "I forget to ask. What'd I say afore you left, and you had the gun on me?"

She smile, sad.

"You said, 'I need this stuff, but it is killing my soul.' So, I shot one jug and left you the other to help finish the job."

"Where'd you go?"

She point opposite camp, other way from the road to town.

"What, just up the road?"

Nod. "A mile."

"Why?"

"You told me to."

"And…" shit. I don't recall what I was gonna say. "And why'd you come here tonight?"

Long second pass. 'Nother.

Now I'm blinkin' too much. Sputterin'. Recallin' that feelin' I was bein' watched in the Hardgrave kitchen. Recallin' my fear at Silas McClellan's — if it wasn't the International's bumper all busted and bloodied, it'd be the Eldorado's.

"Where's the car?"

"Camp."

"So how you know to come here?"

"We followed you every step of every day. I was at the clinic this morning, but other than that, when you were not at camp Joe watched here and I sat on the hill across from McClellan's."

Where she'd know somethin' was goin' on at either place.

"I guess you saw that girl Gretchen and me."

"You are a man. I never thought you were not. Until you quit."

Dosey-do. Here we go.

"All right, Tat. I got to go. You go back to your camp, and I'd like it if you was there — in case I — I'd like us to finish that talk but the Almighty got somethin' for me up here I got to see 'bout."

Tat nod slow. Joe just looks.

I hope it pertain.

I CUT THE WOODS AFTER THE INTERSTATE HEADED FOR THE Hardgrave place. Wonder what this mighty land look like afore Eisenhower did his business with the concrete. Wonder if people drivin' through the locus zone get mean with one another, argue in the vehicle, get cozy with the road rage.

I know the spectre gotta die but I got no idea how it'll happen. Plenty folk in the Bible told the Lord he was mistaken. Time to keep my mouth shut.

Moon's comin' up while I circle the burned barn and approach the house from the orchard. Never see trees so crumbled and broke.

Boots plow grass. Hear my breath. Feel my heart.

I walk.

Gust agin the ear.

At the steps I wait. Don't make sense, me showin' my face here agin. But I get the sense from deep inside this moment is the whole point of my life and lessons so far, and if I turn and walk away, I'll've paid a heavy price without collectin' the prize.

And the prize — the understandin' — is worth collectin'.

I climb to the porch and push open the door and the sound go to the wall and bounce back.

House don't smell like house.

Sound of my boots.

I pass to the kitchen where that spectre work his evil. It's as we left it but the air's regular, like outside.

He ain't here.

I wait for some indication, a nigglin' thought, any sense of the evil was here afore and it's like tryin' to find a chunk of shit in a empty box.

I need a minute, then, illumination:

Devil's hard to kill 'cause I never put him where I can.

Done with this place I head back the door and there on the step like afore is a set of glowin' footprints, sent as a message from my Maker.

I'm noodlin' the insight and prefer to put off any further revelations 'til the last get a little history after it, but the footprints is fadin' and if I want to know, I got seconds to see.

Look back the way I come, then down the porch and 'cross

the hill where Tat say she hid out last time, but the dark is on me and the best I see is shadows in the gray.

Shimmerin' footprints beckon.

Down the slope and 'round like afore, 'cept I can already see what I didn't afore at the end of the golden trail of footprints:

A grave.

I need water so I swallow.

The shoe prints stop at the foot and though they pace and widen, they's fixed in orientation.

A man stood here while another press a gun in his back and drop him in a hole.

The man under the dirt murdered Levi Hardgrave for Silas and his boy Wolfgang, and guaranteed his silence with his life.

CODA

International truck's with the bodies. I start wipin' the wheel and what else I can, but since I ain't workin' my own plan from this point out, I quit. I don't know where I'm goin', so no way in hell the law knowin' I was here'll point 'em where I'm headed next.

I ain't callin' that shot.

May's well leave the truck and bodies as they are.

Tat say her camp was up the road a mile so I walk, ready to jump in the wood if any commotion arise. But it's all crickets.

Been a long while since I fill my belly and the more I ponder the dull ache the less I ponder anything else.

But I'm clear. First time in all my days I'm clear.

Devil's hard to kill 'cause I never put him where I can. No man can kill his demon, and the one he got is the only one that is.

Difference 'tween me and the men I send forward: they serve evil.

I don't serve evil.

Evil serves me.

Moonlight glints off the Eldorado bumper. Tat got the vehicle backed in a loggin' road. Can't see much, but the driver window's down. I pull the handle and the dome light come on.

Tat's inside, passenger seat.

Joe's in back.

Smith on the seat.

I plant a hand on the roof and swing in. Grab Smith, get my ass situated for a drive, flip open the cylinder and nod.

"Gimme one a them under the seat."

Tat reach low and back. Hand me a box of .44 magnum shells.

I take six in hand and drop 'em in the cylinder one by one.

"Where are we going?" Tat say.

"Thataway."

FROM THE AUTHOR

Hello! I appreciate you reading my books—more than you can know. If you've read this far, you and I are fellow travelers. I suspect you sense something is not quite right with the world. It's not as good as it's supposed to be. We human beings aren't as good as our ideals. Yet we prize and want to fight for them.

I do my absolute best to write stories that portray the human situation with brutal transparency, but also I strive to tell stories that are not as bleak as the human condition sometimes seems. There's no limit to the darkness. Light is rare. But it exists, and I hope when you complete one of my novels, you find your values validated.

I'm grateful you're out there. Thank you.

Remember, light wins in the end.

Printed in Great Britain
by Amazon